The Lost Stories
of
J D. Ross Williams

Volume 1

By

John Rossiter

© 2024 John Rossiter

Table of Contents

Forward 5

The Unforgettable Tinkerbelle 6

Pussycat, Pussycat… 10

Chance Encounter 14

A Friend In Need 20

His First Love 23

The Next Empty Chair 26

Dreams And Nightmares 32

A Lesson In Humility 37

Guard Dog's Court Order 44

A Revealing Route 48

Thou Shalt Not Covet 54

A Good Feeling 60

Dulce Domon 66

The Mystery Woman 74

Forward

By
John Rosssiter

This book is part of a series of short stories written by my late Father who sadly died aged 86 after a few years suffering from Dementia.

I was well aware that he was a keen writer and he was a member of The Mold Writers Guild for many years prior to his illness and deterioration. After his death, I was responsible for clearing his belongings and came across an old laptop that he used to write his stories, so I took a look and found hundreds of stories he had written some only a few pages long and others, like this one, a bit longer. In addition he had also written a full novel called "Urchins By The Canal". At the time of writing this, I am in the process of editing and formatting it ready for publishing.

My Father was born in December 1933 in St Asaph, North Wales, but as a toddler he was sent to an orphanage near Liverpool. He joined the Merchant Navy at the age of 15 and worked initially as a cabin boy for the Blue Funnel Line owned by Alfred Holt Ltd. By the time he was 19, he had been around the world 3 times and when he left his last ship in Vancouver, Canada, travelled alone across Canada via the Canadian Pacific Railroad to Halifax Nova Scotia, where he joined another ship to take him back to Liverpool. Now I don't know any 19 year olds today that can say they have done that.

He was a great Father and an inspiration to me and I used to love hearing his tales of exotic ports.

He always wanted to be published but never had the opportunity, so here we are Dad, and you are finally a published writer.

The Unforgettable Tinkerbelle

Mrs Banister had a sleepless night and was feeling tired as she shuffled the children into the lounge. They were as safe there as anywhere but she reminded her eldest, six year old Pattie.

"Now don't you shout at the little ones and just let them play at whatever they want… are you listening to me Pattie?"

She knew that Pattie was prone to order ten months old Julia and four year old Tommy around as if they were lead soldiers but she knew she loved them dearly and would never allow anything to happen to them. As Pattie grew older she found she was too big to sit on Tinkerbelle's back any more. The time came when it was Tommy's turn to ride on Tinkerbelle's back when she had to relinquish her claim on him… and all for a penny whistle…

Tinkerbelle was a toy dog with a smooth textured coat like that of a Teddy bear and stood no more than twelve inches from the floor. He was fixed to a light sturdy tubular frame with four small pink wheels at each corner and a handle at the back to push him along. A little bell hung from a piece of red ribbon around his neck that would tinkle whenever he was wheeled fast or was treated roughly. He had been the constant and intimate friend of lots of children that was evident by the well-worn bare patches on his sides where the little ones had constantly rubbed the insides of their legs against him. His head was also bald where they had patted and comforted him after crashing into the wall.

There was something that endeared him to children that was hard to define. Perhaps they felt sorry for him having only one eye and a stubby tail that had been pulled off at some time and sewn back on again. The tell tale signs of a tug of war between children was evident going by the wisps of straw which protruded out from between the stitches. Perhaps it was the twinkle in his eye or the cheeky expression caused by his turned up nose that they found lovable. It may have been because he was on the same scale as they were in the great wide world of big people that formed a bond with them. Besides, he demanded nothing from the children and was always grateful when they shared a drink of water with him after a good romp around the room. The children's mother was mindful of the fact that it was Tinkerbelle who had always been on hand when the children, as babies, felt the urge to progress from crawling around on all fours to standing up on unsteady legs. He was always there to support them when they attempted their first tentative steps at walking.

Mrs Bannister would often let the children take him for a walk to the corner shop as she realised that, as far as they were concerned, Tinkerbelle was one of the family. The baby in the family would sit proudly on the dogs back while an elder sibling pushed them along. This was a longer and more exciting ride than the sitting room could afford and the thrill for the baby at riding along the pavement was an experience never to be forgotten. Besides, he helped the older ones to stay on their feet and it allowed them more room to push Tinkerbelle at a fast pace so that they could come to an abrupt stop just to hear his bell tinkle...

Tinkerbelle had come into the family from a friend of Mrs Bannister whose five children had all loved him in turn as their very own friend. Even the friend, and her two sisters had played with him when they were children but secretly, it was a wrench to part with him. Although they were all grown up now, their spills and exploits with him were indelibly imprinted on their minds and the memory of him would stay with them throughout their lives. Although Tinkerbelle was showing his age by this time and looking uncared for, Mrs Bannister accepted him in good grace. She put him in the bath and gave him a thorough good scrub and she 'Tut Tutted' to herself and shook her head in despair at the colour of the bath water. When he had dried out in the sunshine his coat looked like new but she had to put some reinforcing stitches in his tail if he was to survive the next tug of war. She saw that his empty eye socket would be a temptation for young children to poke their fingers into his missing eye so she decided to take him to the Doll's Hospital to see if they could replace his missing eye. The Dolly Doctor said he could fix it but Tinkerbelle would have to spend a week in the surgical ward.

When Mrs Banister went to collect him she saw that his new eye was not only a different colour but also it was slightly bigger than the other one. Mrs Banister brought these points to the attention of the Dolly Doctor.
"Yes, of course I can see that Mrs Banister..." he began with a hint of humour in his voice...
"... but you can always explain to the children that the reason is because some naughty child in the past had been cruel to him and had gouged his eye out and besides... " he paused.

"… you could tell them that with one eye bigger than the other he can now see things as good as he ever did before"

There was a pause as Mrs Banister considered the doctor's diagnosis then the penny dropped. She realised that the two built-in defects added interest to the look of the dog and that it could help to engender a feeling of sympathy and a sense of protectiveness in her children. When she gave further thought to the Doctor's words, she was tempted to believe that he had studied child psychology as part of his professional qualifications as a doctor in the Doll's Hospital.

Little Pattie took to him instantly and kissed him constantly because he smelt so new and fresh. He became her sole playmate and in her earlier days, her mother would sit her, bare bottomed, on Tinkerbelle's back so that she could use the potty without encumbrance that was placed behind the settee. Even when her brother Tommy arrived on the scene Mrs Bannister could understand why Pattie was so reluctant to pass him on to Tommy. For long enough, Pattie wheeled her new brother around the room until he realised he could go his own way by propelling himself along with his legs. Gradually but reluctantly, Pattie's physical ties with Tinkerbelle loosened and she knew it was Tommy's turn to share his imagination with him…

It was about that time that Pattie's mother bought her the penny whistle to fill the gap left by Tinkerbelle. She found that it gave her a new air of superiority over Tommy and her newly arrived baby sister Julia. She marched around the house and blew the whistle endlessly to the distraction of her mother and siblings. It was high time to teach her a tune or two to make the noise more bearable so her mother worked on 'Three blind mice' as a starter. This had the effect on Pattie to learn more tunes and soon she was quite good at it. Before long, she had Tommy marching behind her and little Julia riding Tinkerbelle behind him.

Even visiting children had to bide by Pattie's rules and get 'fell in' on parade. The children of the neighbourhood soon referred her to as 'Bossy boots' but strangely enough, the parades appealed more to the local little boys who imagined they were brave soldiers. Some of them even brought their own wooden rifles with them while others brought their younger siblings along to ride on Tinkerbelle's back. Secretly, that wasn't welcome by the Bannister children but they put up with them. Everything went fine for a while until one day when two youngsters wanted to ride on

Tinkerbelle's back at the same time. They started to fight and a tug of war ensued. To Pattie's horror, Tinkerbelle lost his tail in the struggle then the angry children threw him across the floor when he fell over and banged his head against the table leg. Little Julia began to cry while Tommy asserted himself and put Tinkerbelle in the cupboard out of further harms way…

Some years passed and the children had grown up when Pattie and her mother decided on a long overdue clear out. This was prompted by Pattie who was now courting Terry Dalton and whom she was going to marry that August. It had been agreed that the couple should start their married life at the house until they had amassed the deposit for their own place and preparations were being made to that end. They would share everything with the family but Pattie's bedroom was to become their temporary 'marital home'. Mrs Bannister was surprised at the accumulation rubbish that had collected over the years. It fell to her to clear the garden shed out but it turned out to be more than she could cope with. Pattie came to her aid and came face to face with the two cane chairs and the carpet that once adorned her bedroom. Then suddenly, the face of Tinkerbelle came staring out from the jumble. They looked at him in silence and suddenly, they were overcome with a sense of guilt.

"Ah Mum, Look, its poor old Tinkerbelle" she said reverently lifting him off the floor and hugging him. He looked forlorn and evoked some lovely memories of those far off halcyon days when the children were little. There was a long pause as Pattie looked hesitantly at her mother. Pattie brushed him down with her hands and saw that it wouldn't take much to bring him back to his former self. Her thoughts raced ahead and she instinctively knew that it wouldn't be too long before he would have new playmates.

"I think I'll keep him mum… you never know…" she smiled…

"Yes, I think that's very wise Pattie. I do believe he has a lot more love and pleasure to share with little ones. Don't you?"

"No doubt about it Mum and it could be sooner than you think"

He evoked memories in both of them and it was difficult to guess how many other grown-up people still had fond memories of the enigmatic toy dog on wheels… the unforgettable Tinkerbelle and the part he had played in their early childhoods…

The End

Pussycat, Pussycat...

It was Thursday evening and Betty Hallam was alone in the house with Tibbles the cat. She was doing the washing ready to put it out on the line on the morrow. Her mind was occupied with the details of her son's eighth birthday the following Wednesday. The ingredients for the cake had posed a problem insofar as she had saved the family egg ration and had managed to get a handful if raisins and currants but the sugar was the headache. Luckily, her friend and neighbour, Laura Maisefield, came to her rescue and let her have some sugar until she got her next ration the following weekend. She would also need the extra sugar for the custard and jelly that was a great favourite of the children.

Life was bad enough in these frightening and austere times of war but one had to try to mark family milestones such as birthdays. She was determined that her little Richard would have a party and would be able to invite a few of his school friends. The sad thing was that his father wouldn't be home because he was serving in the army somewhere in North Africa. In fact, this would be the second year he had missed his son's birthday so Betty had to double her efforts to make the lad's day.

She went around the house to make sure all the windows were closed and they were all blacked out in case the air raid siren went and she had to leave the house for the shelter. Tibbles was stretched out peacefully in his basket under the corner tall boy where it gave him the best chance of survival in the event of the house being hit by a German bomb. It was unlikely because the German bombers bypassed the town and flew to their targets on a course further east of the town. They were more than likely to be hit by bombs dumped by planes returning to Germany.

It was scout night and Richard would be at the village hall till half past eight. He had been very excited because he was taking his tests for his fire-lighting and woodcutting badges. Betty put on her coat for warmth and glanced at the clock on the mantelpiece. The candle flickered as she noted it was only 7.25 so she sat down and resumed knitting the scarf for Richard's birthday. A neighbour had unravelled a tatty woollen shawl and given Betty what was left of the wool for the scarf. She began to rock gently to and fro humming a lullaby for Tibbles. She thought how fortunate she was, all things considered, but her thoughts turned to her husband Tom who was fighting the enemy somewhere in North Africa.

She had received four letters from him about two months earlier but they were heavily censored to the point as to end up meaningless. Suddenly the cat pricked his ears and Betty knew someone was coming.

She put her knitting under her arm and waited for the knock on the door but it didn't come. Instead, she heard the distinctive monotonous drone of German aircraft in the distance and they were coming closer than usual. She picked Tibbles up in her arms and looking at the ceiling she stroked his head nervously. She blew the candle out and went to the front door to see if Richard was coming. The air raid siren wailed out and Betty realised it was time to run to the shelter. She looked up the street but there was no sign of the boy. She hoped that Hawk, as the scoutmaster was known, had taken his charges to the shelter so she slammed the front door shut. The cat struggled to be free so she placed him in his basket while she took refuge under the table.

By now the planes were almost overhead and bombs were already exploding in their wake. Betty began to say a prayer for the safety of all when suddenly the entire back wall of the house caved in. It was still mainly in one piece reaching a crazy angle. When it stopped moving, there was a deafening silence that was only broken by the anxious meowing from the cat. The poor animal was petrified and Betty tried to get to him but she couldn't move and he was out of reach. She tried to speak slowly and softly to reassure the animal and he knew she was concerned about his safety. As for her, she was almost suffocated by the falling debris and had to breath through the partly knitted scarf to filter out the dust. She was frightened to move a muscle in case she disturbed something and brought the house tumbling down upon them. She didn't know it at the time that her house hadn't been hit directly by a bomb. The reason for the wall going over in one piece was that it was in the van of the blast from a bomb that had exploded nearby. It really was a miracle she was still alive and was evidence to the good workmanship of the people who built the house.

The thought of Richard came to mind and she wondered how his birthday cake had survived in the kitchen cupboard.

"I hope Laura is alright…" she heard herself saying allowed as the cake reminded of her of her friend.

Her thoughts were interrupted by the building creaking under the weight of the slanting wall and she prayed that it wasn't going to collapse in on her. She wanted to live mainly so that she could return the borrowed sugar to Laura. It was very important to her that she didn't let Laura down as she had given up her sugar ration out of the goodness of her heart. There were friends and there were friends she reminded herself but Laura was one of the best.

It took a while for the dust to settle but she couldn't say how long she had been entombed when suddenly she heard voices shouting her name. She knew the rescuers were at hand but as she tried to call out to them she spluttered and coughed with the dust. She managed to call out feebly and hoped they would hear her otherwise, they might move away to rescue other likely survivors. They didn't hear her but they stayed and kept calling her name. She hoped Richard was all right and strained her ears to see if she could hear his voice. Then she realised that all the rescuers wanted to know was whether she was still alive so she had to make a noise of some sort to attract their attention. She fumbled around on the floor and it was with a sense of relief that her hand rested on the dustpan and hand brush. She gripped the brush and began banging on the table for all she was worth.

The men's voices called out her name saying that her rescue was in hand and that she must not give up hope. She hadn't heard the cat meowing for some time so she called his name out but he didn't respond. She called again but still no response and her heart began to sink thinking that Tibbles had died. The rescuers managed to find out where exactly she was in the house and told her to try and stay under the table until they broke through the wall.

The building crunched again and some heavy debris fell. Something solid hit the top of the table, which caused her to flinch violently then everything went quiet outside. Her thoughts were filled with fear that everything would fall in on her and that she would be suffocated. The next thing was she heard Richard's voice calling out nervously;
"Are you okay Mum… it's me, Richard… the men are going to break through the wall now so hold on and you should be out soon"
Betty was overcome by the sound of his voice and tears of joy came to her eyes knowing that he was alive and safe.

The men carefully broke through weakening the slanting structure and causing a huge crack to appear across the wall. They had to work gingerly while talking to Betty all the time to keep her hopes high. She felt the cold fresh air rushing around her as she breathed in deeply through the knitted scarf. Her heart must have missed some beats as she saw the light from one of the rescuers torches. More pieces of debris fell around her and she feared the table wouldn't stand up to the weight but she knew the men couldn't help it. Within the hour they had cleared a way and one of the firemen managed to take hold of her hand and pulled her out through the opening.

She had to hold her eyes shut tightly to keep the blinding daylight out and she realised that she had been trapped all night. It was now Richard's turn to be overwhelmed with relief and he broke down crying out of sheer relief at seeing his mother alive.

"Now then young fella..." said one of the men trying to reassure Richard;

"...that's not like a big scout now is it son... your mother is depending on you now?" he concluded.

Richard wiped his eyes with the cuff of his scout shirt and hugged his mother.

"Where's Tibbles Mum?" he asked with a snivel.

"I think he has gone son because he stopped meowing some earlier in the night" she said clearly distressed by his passing.

She looked around the sea of faces trying to find her friend Laura but she wasn't there.

Just then the cat's green eyes were caught in the beam of the firemen's torch and it was clearly still alive. He started to call it but the animal seemed unable to move. After shifting some rubble he reached in and gently pulled him out.

He handed the bedraggled creature to Richard who lovingly snuggled it against his face.

"Oh pussycat: pussycat; where have you been?" he whispered smiling happily as he held the cat in his arms and stroking him gently...

A neighbour invited them to her house at the other end of the road for a cup of tea and to clean up. As she was led away Betty asked her where her friend Laura was.

"I'm so sorry to have to tell you that Laura's house was one that got bombed and the rescuers said she was dead.

This news set Betty crying again and she felt a sense of guilt not being able to return the borrowed sugar...

The End

Chance Encounter

The road ahead was long and monotonous but Jamie was hoping his final destination would yield the promised prize, i.e. the lasting love of Maisie Connolly. Jamie was heading for the village of Rattley Down which was somewhere ahead on this deserted road. He had only passed his driving test and promised Maisie he would visit her when he bought an old banger. He met up with a man who wanted to sell his ex-army kaki coloured Austen Ten. The man said his name was Keith Brammel and was reluctant to part with 'the old dear' but, because he was emigrating to Australia in three weeks time, well… sadly, she had to go.

Mr Brammel was very plausible and sounded sincere and to be fair, the bodywork on the car looked in very good order. Mr Brammel switched the car lights on then showed Jamie that the windscreen wipers also worked and at the asking price, it was an out and out bargain. Jamie was ignorant as to the pros and cons of motorcars but he was impressed. Mr Brammel had nothing but praise for his reliable steed and Jamie had been convinced it was a bargain. The deal was done and Jamie was handed the logbook then Mr Brammel was gone. Jamie saw nothing wrong by the fact that the name on the logbook was John Allen Bennet. All that concerned him now was that he was the owner of a car that was a certain sign that he was on his way up in the world. Maisie had explained that the road to Rattley Down came to a Y junction and he would have to take the right hand fork that would bring him to the village. He was in two minds as to whether to phone her before he left but the thought of surprising her sounded more romantic. Besides, she didn't really believe he would ever get a car and wasn't convinced he would keep his promise to call on her anyway…

It was only a few years after WWII and the roads were very quiet now that all the military traffic had gone. Jamie couldn't recall when he last saw another vehicle passing in either direction that left him feeling like the king of the road. All was going well and he was thinking he couldn't be that far away from the Y junction when suddenly, his rear near side tyre burst. It had taken him unawares and the car slewed violently brushing against the hedgerow along the side of the road as he tried to bring it to a stop. He sat there shaken for some time trying to compose him self and was content, in the knowledge that, at least, he had a spare wheel in the boot. It wasn't a job he was looking forward to since he had never encountered a blowout but after a while he took the view that it was now or never.

He managed to jack the car up then struggled to remove the wheel that turned out to be a tougher job than he had expected. He felt very disheartened now that he was covered with grease and oil and felt he wouldn't present the ideal suitor to Maisie. He kicked the offending useless wheel and slung it into the boot. When he retrieved the spare wheel, his heart sank when he realised it too was also flat. Perhaps it only needed pumping up, he thought hopefully when it dawned on him he hadn't got a pump. He let out a great sigh of despair and accepted that it was going to be one of those days when nothing would go right.

He wondered how far the nearest public phone box might be and looked up and down the road for likely signs of helpful indications but there were none. His spirits rose when he heard the sound of a distant engine and waited for the vehicle to appear but it came and went in a flash. He cursed himself for not ensuring he was better prepared before setting out but the lovely Maisie Connolly had occupied his thoughts. His wrath now turned towards the man who had sold him the car but the old adage, "There's a sucker born every minute" came to mind…

He was just about to start walking when a car drew up and the driver asked,
"Having trouble?" asked the woman with an Irish lilt.
Jamie felt a great relief that now at least, his troubles could be shared.
"The tyre blew out" he replied as he approached the car hoping to sound knowledgeable about tyre blow-outs.
"Oh dear, that's all you need on this road" said the lady. She went on:
"There is hardly any traffic on this road at the best of times and I'm only here because I've been on business in Caleton.
"Where is the nearest phone box from here? I've forgotten my tools so I'll have to ring a garage" he asked hoping it wasn't too far away.
"Oh, I can do better than that. I'll take you to Willis's garage. He is the only one for miles around and he is very reliable. I'm sure he will have you back on the road in no time at all"
"Well thank you err…Mrs…"
"Just call me Mabel, it'll make things all that much simpler" she said and he found her accent very attractive.

"Well" he began, feeling very aggrieved with himself...

"I'm Jamie Bell... I just discovered that my spare wheel is useless as well" he replied as Mabel's gaze became quite intense.

"It always happens when you least expect it" she said as her gaze remained steadfast on Jamie's face.

She was fascinated by his greenish blue eyes and how expressive they were.

"I wouldn't want to put you out..." he began.

"Oh that's all right; I live quite close to the garage anyway"

Her gaze became more intense as she spoke and their faces came closer together. Jamie became conscious that he was covered with grease and oil. He secretly hoped that wouldn't make her change her mind. She opened the door and invited him to get in.

"There's an old rug on the floor you could put over the seat. I have it there for when I take Chintzy out... she's my dog"

Jamie did as she asked and got into the car.

"Right then, that settles that" she said and the car pulled away from the side of the road.

Suddenly they passed two horses and carts stacked high with hay going in the opposite direction. Mabel put her hand out of the window and waved to the carters who waved back.

"That's old Cody Bates and his son Ely taking the hay back to their barns at their main farm" she said turning to have another look at his eyes.

Jamie was thinking it must be a dull life for such an attractive woman like Mabel living out here in the country but it didn't appear to bother her.

"What brings you to this neck of the woods Jamie?" she asked turning her head slightly.

He was still taken by her lilting accent and radiant looks and thought he could listen to her all day. Besides, he sensed she had a warm disposition that he could live with, always assuming he had to. He was prompted to ask her personal questions but he thought he should not tempt providence further... at least, not before they reached the garage...

The car drew up outside the garage and the young Willis was outside working under a lorry. There was a two-tone Armstrong Siddeley car standing in the small forecourt with a 'for sale' sign in the windscreen. It gave such details as the year 1933, 22 horse power, careful owner and well worth all of £75' Willis got to his feet and rubbed his hands in an oil rag.

"Hello Mabel, what can I do for you?"

"Well, this gentleman, Mr Bell, has had a blow-out back near Panter's Lane and needs you're help Tom"

"You're lucky Mabel was driving past mister otherwise you could have been there all night. There's not a lot of traffic on that road at the best of times"

"And how are you keeping these days Mabel? I see those two young people have settled down in Jack Tate's old house"

"Yes that's right and the man is Jack's youngest son would you believe. They have three lovely boys as well"

Jamie was wondering how long this conversation might go on before the garage man got down to business. He hadn't realised that out here in the countryside everything got dealt with in its own time. Mabel and Tom Willis chatted on about different rural topics before finally Willis addressed Jamie's pressing problem.

"Perhaps I should have brought the wheel with me Tom but there's no room in that car of mine" she said then turned to Jamie.

"Perhaps you would like to come and have some tea while Mr Willis deals with your car Jamie?"

This was music to his ears as he was tired, angry at Keith Brammel, hungry, and already warming towards her.

"I'll drop him off when we have recovered the car Mabel... be about three quarters of an hour" said Willis.

Tom Willis drove Jamie back to the Austen and proved to be an efficient operator. He hooked the stricken car up to the pick-up and in no time at all they were back at the garage. After unhooking the Austen he dropped Jamie off at Mabel's house. He was quite surprised to find that Mabel had two young twin boys.

"So everything is under control now Jamie. Take a seat while mother fixes something for you to eat. The wash place is through there and don't worry about the towels, they are due for the wash anyway" she said.

The house was impressive and he sensed there was a source of money to have furnished it so expensively. The two little boys stood looking up at him and it was clear that they were Mabel's offspring. Jamie was expecting the children's father to make his entrance at any minute but there was no sense of expectancy.

Mabel's mother was quiet and industrious and she made him welcome. It seemed she always picked the children up from the village school and kept the house running to some order. She lived about a mile away in her own house with Mabel's younger brother who was courting Patsy, a local girl. Tom Willis called later that evening to tell Jamie his car was as ready as it would ever be. When Jamie had paid the bill Willis told him that the car's gear box had been doctored and stuffed with heavy oil and sawdust to give the impression that everything was running smoothly, This disclosure secretly enraged Jamie further and he vowed to kill Keith Brammel if ever he saw him again. When the time came to leave, Mabel or her mother would say something to delay his departure and all the time the magnetism between them became stronger. By this time, he was so captivated by her that he found her more irresistible to ignore…

Over the following three months they had a whirlwind romance and the following month they were married. On one beautiful sunny Sunday afternoon, some three years into the marriage, Jamie lay down on the grass intent on getting sunburnt. Mabel had suggested he got a tan to counter his sallow complexion brought about by working as a solicitor all week in a dowdy office. He could hear the voices of the two boys romping around the garden playing cowboys and Indians to the exclusion of everything else around them. He was happy to the 'nth degree as he reflected on his life with Mabel. He had become the 'natural' father of the twins and the father of her baby daughter Jennifer…

Mabel's husband had died suddenly of food poisoning while on a business trip abroad and Jamie knew, understandably, she still missed him. Her family had come together in an extraordinary way and he had never experienced any ill feeling from any of her family, and especially the twins. He felt the heat of the sun on his face and covered it with a handkerchief. He had to admit that Mabel had had a profound effect on him and on his life. He thought of the forthcoming date when he was to become a partner in the new law firm of 'Tennant, Barr and Bell'. He had come a long way and the future with Mabel looked rosy.

His mind wondered and then, his thoughts raked over the circumstances when he first met this charmed lady. He remembered the cheat, Mr Keith Brammel, who had sold him the Austen Ten and how he was going to murder him if he ever caught up with him again but suddenly, he wanted to shake the man's hand and thank him for steering him towards the lovely Mabel. And then he remembered Maisie Connolly and wondered what became of her. He lingered on his fortuitous chance encounter with Mabel and wondered where he would have been now if he had taken the other path to Maisie Connolly and Rattley Down….?

The End

A Friend In Need

During the night there was a heavy fall of snow that tended to dampen the dawn chorus of the birds and the bleating of the sheep in the fields. It was still early as Jack Hamilton lay fully awake in his bed. The morning sunlight was defused by the closed cream curtains leaving the room pleasantly bright. He was an early morning person and would have normally jumped out of bed but there was something odd about this morning. He wouldn't have thought anything about it if his ex wife Julia had been lying beside him but she had been lured away from him eighteen months earlier by the younger Allan Partridge.

Like Hamilton, Partridge had not only been a member of the business community but was also his closest friend. Not that Partridge was in the same league as Hamilton whose business was buying and selling thousands of tons of crude oil while it was still on the high seas. He still considered Partridge had stolen Julia from him by abusing his long standing friendship. Partridge had even offered Julia a Directorship in his company that she accepted and which, most probably, finally persuaded her to leave Jack and join him.

Both men were prominent members of the Groves Cricket Club where Hamilton was well known as a good sportsman. He secretly nurtured this *persona* simply because he could afford to and because it raised his prestige and made him feel a better man. When Julia left, him nobody was surprised when he was reported as saying that "…the best man won..."

"Typical of the man" said an acquaintance in the bar.

"That's Hammie to a T all right" said another.

His reaction was predictable… Win some lose some… Play up, play the game and all that… was the general perception of him. That was over eighteen months ago and to all intents and purposes Partridge was seen to have won the day. The two men would still meet socially at the old venues and Hamilton would often enquire…

"How is business Allan?" and

"We seem to be seeing you less and less these days…" and

"How is your lovely wife keeping…You must know that the members would like to see more of you and Julia"

Partridge would invariably answer,

"Oh! Business is moving ahead at a steady rate and Julia is her usual self" he would add.

The sporting and, to some extent, the predictable Hamilton was bound to answer…

"Ah Good, Good; we really would be glad to see her at the club more often…

These encounters, together with Hamilton's interest in their welfare, evoked in Partridge a sense of guilt at the man's genuine understanding and his apparent forgiveness. The club members in general admired him in the absence of any hard feelings he may have shown towards Partridge as well as the equanimity he had displayed in the face of all the heartache and loss of his dear friend and wife Julia.

Like most businessmen, Partridge always painted a rosy picture of the state of his business. His main supplier, Wade Bros Limited, had themselves been experiencing difficult trading conditions causing work to dry up. Wade Bros began to press Partridge harder on his outstanding account while always assuring him that business was bound to pick up in the near future. His debts were now exceeding his assets and there was a real danger of Wade Bros Limited making him bankrupt. As a temporary measure to remain solvent, Partridge was forced to raise capital on the title deeds of his grand home. He made strenuous efforts trying to maintain an outward stability in the hope of a turn up in business activity. His debts kept rising while an expectant improvement in the business seemed a long time coming.

As the pressures of debt increased his private life was showing signs of falling apart. Julia had seen the writing on the wall and could see that her life style was threatened. One at a time she saw the domestic staff being sacked in an effort to economise on the household expenditure. In the event, she ended up having to do the cooking, which wasn't her forte, and the general cleaning which left her feeling very demeaned. It reached the point when she felt she was no more than a skivvy in her own home and plans to preserve her future began to germinate in her mind.

One morning, after an unusually heavy sleep, he got up still feeling groggy. He called out to Julia but there was no sign of her. He took a slug of whiskey in an effort to clear his head but he soon realised she had deserted him. She had cleared the house of everything of any value and driven off in his Range Rover. He looked about him forlornly and couldn't accept that she had turned her back on him. All his troubles seemed to be tumbling down on his head together and he suddenly realised at he didn't even own the house anymore. He could never have envisaged Julia deserting him and that was the last straw. His world was crumbling around his ears and the outlook was bleak. He realised he would have to answer for his debts in the bankruptcy court and face the humiliation of failure in the glare of publicity. It was all too much to bear and he broke down sobbing in the chair. He was not seen for over a week and a few days later the police had to break into the house where they found him dead on his bed. He had chosen to take a massive overdose of poison rather than suffer any further ignominy and disgrace in the eyes of the business community…

Hamilton was out of bed in a flash, full of life and ready to confront the challenges of the day. He drew the curtains open allowing the sunshine to flood into the room. The lawns and fields looked rich and green while the birds and the sheep chirped and bleated in the warmth of the morning. As the owner of Wade Bros Limited, he was to be a key witness later in the morning at the coroner's inquest into the death of Allan Partridge. When questioned by the Coroner, he told the court that when he heard that Wade Bros Limited was experiencing trading difficulties, he realised how that would in turn affect his friend's, the diseased Allan Partridge's business, so he decided to buy it and leave Jack Wade, the only surviving brother, to run the business on his behalf.

His attention was drawn to a marmalade Tomcat just noticeable under a bush and which appeared to be having difficulty moving with the grace of a predator. The birds must have sensed something was amiss with the cat as it remained motionless and they showed no signs of being intimidated or fooled by it. Even though the cat sat motionless the birds hopped and flew about in front of him in seemingly mock derision. Hamilton smiled wryly knowing that the birds had the upper hand for the present but the cat would recover and would surely have his day. He was reminded of his fellow cricket club members and of Partridge in particular. They had all sincerely believed he was the fountain of forgiveness but just as the birds would learn a salutary lesson at the cost to their lives when the cat recovered so too would the members of the cricket club realise that you don't become wealthy by being predictable…

The End

His First Love

Father Edwin Fowler heard the door click then waited for the confessor to begin unburdening his soul. As he listened to the nervous shallow breathing on the other side of the small partitioned paneled window he became aware of the fragrance of a scent he recognised as Capture and realised it must be a woman. He knew of one particular young lady who used it on occasions but his suspicion would only be confirmed when she spoke.

"You may begin when you are ready" he said hoping to prompt the confessor but there was only the breathing.

"Is that you Jane?" he asked firmly hoping to force the issue...

Father Edwin Fowler had been at St Mary's since he left the seminary two years earlier at the age of twenty three. He was six feet one inch tall with deep blue eyes and a head of short cropped hair. His athletic build and strong jaw line had not gone unnoticed by the female members of the congregation and he was often the topic of their conversations. Even the ageing parish priest, Father Morton, feared that young Edwin had many hurdles to overcome.

Jane Irving was sixteen years old at the time of his arrival and even then, the young Father Edwin, as he was usual referred to, had been captivated by her large warm smoldering brown eyes. In the two years since then she had matured and had let her hair grow down her back adding further to her feminine allure. To his surprise, he felt safe and comfortable in her company but the thought that she was falling in love with him didn't enter his mind. As time went on however his own feelings for her began to change and something within him stirred each time they met. Soon, he suspected he was falling in love with her and he had to learn to avert his eyes from her ...... beauty. She always brought to mind the Dean at the seminary who lectured on the subject of temptation and the vulnerability of the male species in the broader scheme of things. The Dean would advise his students on what steps might be taken to avoid falling by the wayside.

Jane's father was the local jeweller and often advised the church council on financial matters. Together with his wife and two sons, the Irvings were a devout Catholic family. Father Edwin had noticed that only recently Jane had changed to the more prominent aisle pew for Sunday

Mass where she became a constant distraction. As young as she was, she had already joined that that small dedicated band of women who dusted, polished and arranged the flowers in the church just to be near him. Edwin sensed that she was that hurdle which was so often referred to by the lecturer in the seminary. He had come to realise that, where once he used to pray in those silent moments before falling sleep, his mind was now filled with thoughts of the lovely Jane. The more he tried to banish her image from his mind the further his restlessness took him into the early hours of the morning. The zeal of his priesthood was beginning to lose its fire and there was a growing inner struggle between the spirit and the flesh. At first, he followed the advice of the college lecturer by avoiding possible encounters with temptation but soon he found excuses to be in the church especially when the flowers were being changed. He would kneel in a pew near the front with missal open just to watch Jane's poetic movements as she went about the altar arranging the flowers. Then, as she was on the point of leaving he would approach the altar under the guise of complimenting her on the floral display just to be closer to her.

A pink bowed ribbon held her hair in place like a flowing mane and he couldn't help thinking of her as a young spring filly, wild, beautiful and exciting. He eyes now haunted him while the sound of her quiet voice sent tingles through his veins. She stopped on the other side of a vase of roses which stood on a pedestal and their eyes met between the blooms. Edwin knew he was in love with her as a deep passion rose within him. Suddenly, he had a great urge to kiss her and take hold of her flowing hair but the nearest he got was to put a fatherly arm around her shoulders and walk with her to the church door. It was at that moment he knew he was falling at the first major hurdle of his priesthood. All sorts of doubts regarding his vocation welled up to the surface. He felt torn between questions of loyalty, betrayal and confusion between his heart, mind and soul. Was he about to desert his faith, this congregation and his once closely held religious convictions? He realised he loved her deeply and was in no doubt Jane was his for the asking and yet he was angered by his own weakness of will.

People noticed how they reacted when they met and it was not long before rumours gathered pace. Not wanting to see Jane getting hurt and fearing a scandal, Edwin confided in Father Morton. He arranged for Edwin to return to the seminary for a three week retreat to renew and strengthen his vocation. The discipline in the college was more conducive to prayer and meditation but in moments of idleness he was still haunted by his heart's desire to be close to Jane. He could still see her in his mind's eye moving like a dream across the altar at St Mary's with her long hair swinging from hip to hip and her smile lighting up those smoldering brown eyes.

After much soul searching he spoke to the Dean about his feelings and suggested it would be easier if he was sent to another parish. The Dean in his wisdom explained that temptation was not exclusive to St Mary's and must be met head on wherever it was encountered. Edwin accepted he would have to return to St Mary's and face up to his love for Jane. The question was whether he had the will to resist the temptation and follow the path of celibacy or whether the weakness of the flesh would culminate with the lovely Jane in his embrace. The vision of God battling with Satan for his soul was a constant visitor to his troubled mind…

Her voice was closer now and by the dim light above his head Father Edwin could just make out the fain outline of her delicate features behind the small paneled window in the partition. He then opened it to form a frame around Jane's face. She was only inches from him and he was sorely tempted to kiss her inviting lips. They looked deep into each others eyes for what seemed an eternity and he prayed for the strength to resist the gloating grin of Satan.
"It is highly irregular for me to confront a confessor like this, Miss Irving, but as much as I will always respect and think highly of you, it would be easier for both of us if you would let Father Morton hear your confessions in future"

As he closed the panel window he felt a pang of sadness in his heart but thanked God for giving him the strength and purpose, which enabled him to walk away from this momentous temptation. Perhaps he would be a better priest for having resisted the powerful temptation of falling in love with such a beautiful woman but the unrequited love would haunt him forever. From then on he vowed to strengthen his commitment to the life-long service of the Catholic Church. After all, his priestly vocation had always been his first love…

The End

The Next Empty Chair

With admirable promptitude, Kate entered the common room of the Fern Lodge old people's home on 3.30. She went into the small kitchen and put the kettle on then set the cups and saucers out ready for the resident's afternoon tea. She was the youngest at sixty even years of age and secretly felt she was the most reliable person to get things underway. Besides, it was nice to have something to do that not only added interest but also responsibility and structure to her life. She sat in her chair facing the door, lit a cigarette and waited for the others to trickle in.

Right on 3.45, 71 year old Mabel, a surviving twin sister, and three times widowed Esther, entered the room and sat in their usual chairs. They were always together and it seemed as if Mabel, unconsciously, used Esther as a proxy for her deceased twin sister Deirdre while Esther must have felt the loneliness of being without a husband. They bid Kate good afternoon and commented on the rainy weather. Another five minutes passed then Wilfred, 75, arrived leaning heavily on his walking stick.

"Where is everybody?" he asked glancing around the room as if surprised'
"Well, Harold and Mrs. Anderson won't be coming down because they are not feeling too good but the others will be here shortly, Wilf" was Kate's usual reminder.
"I saw Beckwith going out this morning with his youngest granddaughter but I expect he'll be back in time for tea" said Esther,
Beckwith was a tall elegant looking 92 year old ex railway assistant stationmaster. He looked very distinguished in his silver rimmed spectacles but they did nothing for his failing eyesight. His granddaughter's routine was to take him home to her place as often as possible to spend time with her family.

Just then, 74 year old ex army bandsman Teddy, nicknamed the whistler, entered with Molly, a retired nurse aged who was coming up to her 86 birthday and 70 year old ex miner Little John. They filed into the room and took up their usual places around the wall. Little John just collapsed into his chair gasping for breath. AS soon as he had recovered he lit up a cigarette and threw one to Kate. The empty chair next to his used to be occupied by his drinking and smoking pal Baz but he had passed away only ten days earlier. Nobody had sat in his chair since and it was likely to remain empty until the room was used for some kind of social function. Perhaps the residents secretly felt it would be tempting fate too far to sit there so they gave it a wide berth…

Daisy was always very proud of her war service as a sergeant in the Observer Corps. She had always insisted on marching to the local cenotaph on Remembrance Day with the other veterans right up until she began to feel the weight of her years. Kate relieved her of a packet of chocolate biscuits and Beckwith referred to the weather.

"I think its time to wet the tea" said Kate as she rose to her feet and went into the kitchen followed by Esther and Mabel.

The others waited expectantly then 69 year old Donald, 75 year old Alice, an ex land army girl who still had a fetish for large flowery wide-brimmed hats and Mary with the fading memory, entered to room and took their places. There were lots of well-practiced smiles and afternoon greetings. Mabel looked back into the room from the kitchen to see who had arrived and more cups were filled accordingly.

After a long silence, there was a rush to say something by a number of them but it was Molly who scored first.

"Did you see the picture in this morning's paper of that poor old woman who was beaten senseless by burglars in her own home?"

There was an instant response:

"Terrible"

"They should be horse whipped"

"Poor soul"

"I'll bet they get away with"

"They wouldn't 'ave done that to an old lady in my day" said ex police sergeant Donald in an uncompromising voice.

"For one thing, we'd have sussed them out long before such ideas took root. One visit to the police station and they would have been taught a life-long lesson in good social be'aviour" he added authoritatively

As a young miner, Little John had first hand experience of the police when they took him to the local police station on a number of occasions for being tipsy. He never forgot the experience and remembered he was treated with anything but kid gloves.

"I have known prisoners being thrown out of the police station with broken arms, bloody noses and swollen eyes" he said with the sole

27

intention of letting Donald know what everyone knew at the time i.e. That once the police got their hands on you in the confines of the police station there was no knowing what they would do to you. Not only that but, it was pointless trying to complain because they just denied all knowledge of it and the establishment believed them.

"Yes well, you 'ave to remember that in those days the cells were usually down the cellar so it wasn't surprising that prisoners often fell down the stone stairs and hurt themselves. You can hardly blame the police for that" Donald replied sounding well practiced with his explanation.

The ladies took him at his word but the men knew different.

"The trouble is that youngsters today seem to do as they like 'cause they know their social workers will make sure that nothing happens to them" said Daisy with traces of her army sergeant days.

"They aught to be birched" she added.

"I have to admit that I never hit any of my children" said Little John philosophically.

"Why? Didn't you believe in taking them to task when they did something wrong?" asked an irate Donald with a scowl on his face.

"Oh no, it was nothing like that Donald… it was just that I couldn't run as fast as the blighters" he quipped, tongue in cheek.

Teddy roared with laughter and the ladies laughed noting the mischief in Little John's eyes.

There was a brief lull as concerned minds reflected on the suffering of the burglar's victim. Teddy began quietly to whistle the hymn 'Abide with me'. He had hardly got through ten bars when Daisy returned to the weather.

"Did you hear that thunder and lightening last night, wasn't it dreadful?"

Several ladies responded together then silence fell again but Teddy continued to whistle the hymn.

"I do so get frightened by the flashing lights sometimes" said Molly.

"You're not on your own my dear…" assured Little John "… 'cos I always get scared too. My advice to anyone who gets frightened by the thunder and lightening is to do what I always do…" he paused and all heads turned to him fully expecting to hear an original pearl of wisdom fall from his lips.

"Next time you get frightened just shout for your mum then dive under the bedclothes…" he added with a glint of mischief in his eyes.

The very thought of Little John doing just that brought howls of laughter while the quiet and slightly hard of hearing Alice thought of her own childhood.

"Ah, how true, how true" she sighed wistfully.

Just then Kate and Esther emerged from the kitchen each holding a cup of tea which they served to Teddy and Little John. They were followed by Mabel who gave each person a side plate and offered them chocolate biscuits. Soon, everybody was served and the conversation was buoyant. Suddenly, there was a lull which lingered as minds were trawled for topics new. Teddy had turned the music pages in his mind and started to whistle Schubert's Ave Maria.

Kate lit a cigarette and out of habit threw two towards Little John and Bazil's empty chair. It was only then she realised Baz had gone forever and Little John threw one back. He lit up then coughed in a vain attempt to break the silence but he only managed too provoke his long ill treated lungs. He started to cough uncontrollably while everyone waited for him to regain his composure. Teddy stopped whistling and Molly, the ex nurse, went over and patted him on the back.

Wilfred couldn't help thinking of the bookmaker's odd and just as Little John had regained control he chirped in;

"I wouldn't cough like that while passing the bookmakers if I was you John… you'd get lousy odds" he said managing to maintain a deadpan expression on his face.

All the men, including Little John appreciated the joke but the ladies could only offer puzzled smiles.

The time was now twenty to five and the lulls in the conversation were getting longer and more drawn out leaving the stage to Teddy's whistling. People cast their eyes towards the floor and began to fidget with their fingers. One could almost feel the ageing minds being trawled at depth to come up with something new and interesting to say.

The forgetful Mary, looking suddenly alert, suggesting she had a brain wave began to speak.

"Wasn't that errr… errr…" she was struggling to get the words out before the vision in her conscious mind began to fade. She was losing the thread almost immediately as the normal mental processes began to lose function. Out of sheer frustration she began to stab at the air in front of her with a shaky forefinger. She was trying to keep track of the mental picture in the forefront of her mind.

"You know, that err… err…" she was fighting desperately to hang on to the fading thought. Kate was next to her and tried to help.

"Did you want to say something about the picture in this morning's Post, Mary?" she asked with great understanding.

"No, no, the err… the err… you know…" then suddenly blurted out with great relief;

"That's it, that thunder and lightening last night"

The words were rushed out and she breathed a sigh of relief and sank back into the chair exhausted.

"Where you frightened then Mary?" asked Esther. Mary's eyes glazed over again and everyone knew the mental picture had gone. Silence fell over the room and everyone understood. Teddy took his cue and began to whistle "Eternal Father strong to save"

Esther suddenly remembered there was still a half pot of tea left.

"Would you like another cup of tea Donald?" she asked.

He nodded then Mary changed the subject. "Did you know that Mrs Walters is getting buried tomorrow afternoon?"

"Oh dear I didn't even know she had died" said a shocked Daisy who used to live a couple of doors away from her some years earlier.

"Is that son of hers still living with her?" she added.

"I don't think so"

"Didn't he marry that girl from Hooler Street?" asked Teddy taking a rest from his whistling.

Nobody was conversant with the details of the topic and it lost momentum.

"Here's Beckwith coming up the path" said Kate straining her neck to see out of the window.

All eyes turned to the door expectantly but Beckwith's daughter led him directly to his flat explaining that he wasn't feeling too well.

"There's still some tea left in the pot" Esther reminded everyone.

It was twenty past five and almost time to go. Kate, Esther and Molly collected the cups and saucers and the others began to trickle out in much the same order as they had arrived. Teddy was able to give full vent to his music and could be heard doing justice to the march, "Blaze away" as he marched along the corridor to his flat. Everyone was now left ready for tomorrow's afternoon tea and Kate was last to leave. She closed the window, switched the lights off and looked around the empty room. She was still feeling self conscious about throwing the cigarette for the departed Bazil and as she closed the door behind her she couldn't help wondering which would be… the next empty chair…

The End

Dreams And Nightmares

Mrs Liz Arnley was in the kitchen preparing dinner for her husband Jeremy who would arrive from the office at 5.30pm. Her eighteen month old son William was in the sitting room playing with a mountain of toys which kept him occupied and out of mischief. Liz would pop in from time to time to check on him as and when the dinner preparations allowed or to switch the television over to the child's favourite programme. She had eliminated most of the likely hazards in the room over the period of Tracy's baby years. Tracy was her four year old daughter who was presently playing in the children's cottage at the far end of the garden. The little girl had bright blue eyes with a faint sprinkling of freckles that matched her light golden hair. Her mother would take great care to comb the silk tresses out then work them into one long plait which was then adorned with pink silk ribbon.

Jeremy had built the little cottage for Tracy out of solid wood then painted ivy and roses around the door. It had a red tiled roof and a tall grey chimney pot and had a window on each side of the door. Liz had added the woman's touch by hanging two animal pictures inside and flower patterned curtains on the windows. Jeremy had got the idea from one of Tracy's colouring books when she was still only a toddler and going by the intervening time it had proved a worthwhile investment. It soon became Tracy's second home but only Jeremy had any idea why it held such an attraction for the little girl. Jeremy always had an inkling that Tracy was one of those children who would be quite content to spend a lot of time seemingly playing on her own. In fact, she was always in the company of her friends who were more often than not invisible to anyone else. Jeremy knew from his own childhood that the Wendy cottage would be the ideal place for Tracy to meet and talk freely with her secret friends without being bothered by skeptical and nosy grown-ups.

There was a row of trees at the back of the Wendy cottage which grew along the boundary wall of the property. At each side of the cottage was a lilac tree… one white and the other lilac. In front of them were several differing rose bushes which always appeared to be in bloom and which seemed to keep the Wendy cottage in a permanent state of summer. There was a short crazy paved pathway with rustic palings on each side leading up to the brown front door. Of course, the magical perception of this mini wonderland was all in the mind of a little child… well, that is what Liz thought. Little did she realise how real this world was to Tracy and how deeply the child was involved with its inhabitants. In the child's earlier years, Liz used to creep up to the cottage and listen to Tracy talking to herself but somehow the little girl always knew she was there. She had begun to get worried about this behaviour and had confided her fears in Jeremy. He had dismissed her concern by saying;

"Oh Liz, you are worrying about nothing. Lots of children have secret and imaginary friends and it's not for us to shatter their worlds. Besides…" he paused and hoping to allay her fears he admitted shyly; "… I had a secret friend when I was little but I grew out of it… I think" This was the first Liz had heard this and it amused her. "What sort of friend did you have then?" she teased. She could see that Jeremy was suddenly self conscious so she teased him further. "Well, what was his name then?" she persisted. He felt foolish, now that he had let the cat out of the bag and he tried to close the subject by saying he had forgotten but Liz was having none of it. "Oh, come now Jeremy, you are not trying to tell me that you have forgotten your closest childhood friend, surely" He knew by the tone of her voice that she was not going to give up as easily as that so he relented. "You won't laugh if I tell you… promise?" he pleaded. "Just tell me his name Jeremy, that's all I want to know"

She had him on the run now and he knew the die was cast… he would have to reveal all so he took the bull by the horns. "Well, for a start, it wasn't a he or, it was an 'It'"

Liz folded her arms believing she could be in for a long story. "Well, what was 'Its' name then…? Come on, tell me. I want to know" she coaxed.

There was a long pause and Liz and Liz had to keep up the pressure. "Well, I'm waiting Jeremy; what was 'Its' name?"   "Wumbeloom" he mumbled through clenched teeth but she didn't hear him clearly. "You'll have to speak slower than that and more clearly Jeremy" He knew she was teasing him and he knew she was going to drag the whole story from him.

"Wumbeloom" he blurted out.
"Wumbel… what?" she asked as she began to break into a laugh. "You heard Liz: I'm not repeating it again" he said with a tone of finality in his voice. "Well, what sort of an 'It' was it Jeremy. I mean, what did it look like?" He tried to avoid answering her but she was adamant.

"Well, if you must know it was a green and pink lady bird which had two long feelers and no legs"

The image this description conjured up sent Liz into howls of laughter. After a while she thought he might be stringing her along and she stopped to ask him to confirm he was speaking the utter truth. "Well of course I'm telling you the truth… don't I always tell you the truth?" he replied throwing the onus on to her.   "Well if Wumbeloom had no legs how did 'It' move around?" she asked thinking the question would make him think harder.   "Oh, that was no problem because 'It' moved around on eight little wheels" he replied without giving the question a second thought. "You can't have a lady bird which has wheels instead of legs Jeremy… everyone knows that" she said trying to illicit more information about this strange creature.   "Oh but you can Liz because Wumbeloom used to let me sit on his back and give me rides around my bedroom" Jeremy replied with a good deal more confidence…

This tale from a child's mind intrigued her and she wondered how big Wumbeloom actually was if it could let a little boy ride around on his back. He explained that Wumbeloom was a good foot across its back and only for its colour it could have been likened to a big tortoise. The last laugh was on Liz as Jeremy managed to convince her that many young children believed in, and even invented, little friends but they eventually grew out of it. As a result of that conversation Liz was quite happy to leave little Tracy alone in her private world in her Wendy cottage…

Tracy's birthday fell at the end of March when her secret world came to life. At the first signs of spring her friends would set up home at the cottage and would stay until the weather began to get colder in the late autumn. There were five of them and they had told Tracy seasons before that they belonged to the Teppi Tribe of Mynutines. The Mynutines were a race of tiny elfish people who seldom grew more than a quarter of an inch tall but were perfect in every other respect. Elves in general were known to be malevolent in character who often stole children and left one of their malignant 'changelings' in its place. They usually had haggard expressions on their drawn faces and the locks of their hair were clotted together. It has to be said however that the Teppi Tribe were quite the opposite and were a gifted and cultured people. As far as Tracy was concerned they were kind, generous and always helpful to their friends. The spoke a language of their own called Ploon and had the power to allow certain little humans to understand them.

As soon as she felt the weather getting warmer Tracy would leave the cottage window open so that her little friends could fly in as soon as they arrived.
"Fly in through the window?" did I hear you say. "The answer is yes; that is to say the Mynutines had trained dragon flies and butterflies to ferry them across long distances. They were a loving people and were led by the enigmatic Podjit the Elder who had lived many years and whose white silky beard touched down to his shins. His long white wispy hair flowed down his slightly stooped back which caused the others to refer to him as an Ancient... and great honour and privilege accorded only to those revered by the Mynutines. Podjit the Elder was the fountain of wisdom of the group while his son Pahli was the man of action.

The lovely Velba was his wife and they had two offspring, a male called Oblae and a female they called Emlet. Velba did all the cooking and sewing and tended to the needs of the group. Emlet was in charge of the collectors such as the bees and butterflies whose job it was to collect pollen and honey which she stored in spent acorn shells. These were stored behind webs which were specially woven for the purpose by the wood spider who gave his services free. This cache of food was used to tide the family over rainy days when Podjit had decreed that no collector should work out in the rain on their behalf.

Oblae had no time to waste as he had to train newly captured woolly bears in the art of carrying elves over rocky ground. It took a long time for these hair caterpillars to get used to their harnesses and submit to the will of a riding elf. Once they had acquired the knack of answering the reins they were quite happy to serve their benign masters. The reins were strong and were made by Velba from the long silken web threads of the field spider. This was very important because the family would stride their mounts and set off in high summer travelling over rough terrain in search of ripe berries.

They were an industrious people but anything Tracy could do for them was always appreciated. Tracy would often take of spoon of chunky marmalade down to the Wendy cottage when the little people would eat their fill then settle down to sleep. At other times, she would search the kitchen for a handful of mixed fruit such as currants and raisins or, better

35

still, some brown sugar which was a favourite of the Mynutines. She loved to share everything with them and on special occasions she would sing for them to the accompaniment of Podjit on his violin and Pahli on the flute... It was getting late and Tracy said she was feeling hungry. Velba wanted to share their honey with her but the little girl said that even if she emptied all the acorn shells of their honey she would still be hungry. She said she would have gone home earlier for her tea only her mother would put her to bed and she wanted to stay up. "Bye, bye," she called then ran up to the house and tucked into her fruit cake and ice cream. Her father had returned home from the office and was sitting at the table reading the evening paper. He and Liz then watched their little girl eat ravenously. "And how is Emlet today Tracy?"

The little girl was so hungry that she could only answer between gulps.
"Velba said it was getting late and as they were going out blackberry picking tomorrow they had to get to bed early so that's why I have come home" she said while not losing any interest in her ice cream. "I do hope the blackberry picking won't be too strenuous for old Mr Podjit" said Jeremy. Tracy was too involved with her ice cream to answer.

Later that evening when the two children were long in bed Liz said with some concern in her voice;
"How long do you think it will be before Tracy begins to forget about the Wendy house and its association with the little people Jeremy"

There was quite a pause before Jeremy answered. "I wouldn't be too much in a hurry for Tracy to forget about her friends Liz. You see, I look at it like this. We all have to get through childhood one way and another. The only trouble is that for far too many children their young lives are remembered as black frightening nightmares. For the lucky ones childhood is recalled as a permanent happy daydream which was going to last for ever and ever... look at me for instance" he joked. They both laughed and Jeremy kissed her gently on her lips. He had reassured her of the innocence of the little friends in the child's imagination and that everything would turn out for the best in the end...

The End

A Lesson In Humility

The five children and their pet dog Timmy were minding their own business as they walked along the pavement. A little way ahead the three bullies from the grammar school were sitting on the bench waiting for possible victims to pass by so that they could insult them and even assault them providing they thought they could get away with it.

"Look who is waiting on the bench Rusty" said Wingy without a trace of fear in his voice.

He had acquired the nickname Wingy because of the particular way he held his arms when running.

The older boys were slouching over the seat like jellyfish making sure there was no room for anyone else. Their long school scarves were wrapped around their necks then trailed down over their knees. They looked contemptuously at the youngsters and Blashford seemed to have a permanent sneer on his face. The truth of the matter was, if it be known, that the three grammar school boys were out and out snobs. They felt that their lofty superior attitude towards the lower classes, particularly those from the council houses, was the way to preserve the long and distinctive historic connections their own school had with royalty. They would never in a million years describe themselves as arrogant...

The two girls, together with the boys, were pupils of Holy Cross Roman Catholic School and it was true to say that there was no love lost between the pupils of both schools. Lizzie Makin and Cathy Blaby, were all for going out into the road and giving the bullies a wide berth but David took hold of their hands and held them on the pavement.

"Don't let them see that you are scared of them because they'll only come after you twice as hard" he told them holding their hands firmly.

The boys were about three years older than Wingy and his friends and were pupils at The King's Grammar School. Perhaps that was why they considered themselves a cut above the other school children and thought that they were the crème de la crème of the village. They had been eating bags of broken biscuits obtained for half price from Looper's biscuit factory and making derogatory remarks at their chosen victims as they passed by. As the five younger friends were passing, the bullies started making jibes at them but they stood their ground and gave as much as they got. The big one, Francis Blashford, who was the undoubted ring leader, sat on the end of the bench. He stood up leaving his biscuits on the seat and inflated his chest with the intention of intimidating the younger children.

He then proceeded to poke Wingy in the shoulder with his stiffened forefinger... a habit he had copied from one of the grammar school teachers, but Wingy was having none of it. He was the short-tempered one of the group and was quick to react. He pivoted around with speed and socked Blashford in the eye. Of course, he was smaller than Blashford and had to jump off the ground just to reach him. Blashford's expression changed to one of dismay, as he couldn't believe that Wingy had the audacity to strike one of his betters but he certainly knew now. The other two, Barney Swanson and Ian Wilson, who were hurling insults at them jumped up and started assaulting Rusty while grinning like Cheshire cats. David steered the girls away then joined in the fracas. He took on Wilson and the three younger boys struck while they were in close range then moved away niftily.

While Blashford had been pontificating, Timmy had muzzled his way through the side of the bench and stealthily took hold of Blashford's bag of biscuits. He slipped away just as Barney Swanson caught sight of him with the bag between his teeth. Blashford became indignant when he realised the dog had taken his biscuits and started shouting after the animal. Timmy was ambling along intent on hanging on to his booty while the three bullies gave chase. The faster they ran the faster went Timmy while the younger children laughed and cheered the dog on. Not wanting to be outdone by a scruffy dog, they started to throw stones at Timmy and he instinctively put more and more distance between him and them. Alas, Blashford was a vindictive character and had a long memory and Timmy was a marked dog...

It was a hot sunny day and the five friends were at a loss as to what to do to pass the time away. There were many questions and much debate as to their options and it was Rusty who suggested they go for a swim in the Bluebell Pool in Asterley Woods. That was agreed and they all took swimming trunks, of sorts, but it was left to the girls to bring towels which they would share with the boys then they all set off for a swim and paddle. Timmy wasn't going to be left out so he trailed along behind them. They had been there several times in the past and it was a place where there was nobody to shout at them. Lizzie's mother warned her daughter on the way out to take care and behave herself.

It took them all but twenty minutes to reach the woods and experience the peace of the place. The silence was broken only by the bird song as the shafts of sunlight filtered through the towering trees. It was awe-inspiring and not unlike a great natural cathedral with a path as the aisle leading to the pool. Their lives were too well ordered but this gave them the opportunity to rebel against society's imposed order as they preferred to meander quietly through the trees towards the pool.

Timmy was in his element and was at a loss with so many trees to visit and leave his scented messages for other passing canines. Suddenly he stopped dead in his tracks and pricked up his ears. Cathy drew the attention of the others to the dog and they all stopped to listen intently. Timmy took several tentative steps forward and the children looked in the direction he was pointing. They moved on cautiously and as they neared to pool they heard voices. The dog found heaps of clothes at the rivers edge and it seemed the revelers had disrobed here and then ran along the river to the pool. The children examined the clothes and found they were Kings Grammar School uniforms. Wingy and Cathy went ahead to see what was happening at the pool and saw three boys splashing in the water. They saw their towels on the edge of the pool and the temptation to take them away was strong but they resisted. They went back to the others and reported that the clothes belonged to none other that Barney Swanson, Ian Wilson and Francis Blashford… the grammar school terror gang.

Immediately, Lizzie's imagination began to work overtime and the others guessed, by the broad mischievous smile on her face, what she was thinking.

"Your not thinking of hiding their clothes are you Lizzie?" asked Rusty realising what an opportunity they had been presented with.

Lizzie nodded her head slowly and deliberately and they all started to laugh at the very idea. Wingy cautioned silence as each of them gathered up the items of clothing and shoes then stealthily retreated back into the thick of the woods. They found a suitable hollow in the ground a fair distance away and placed the clothes in it then covered them over with leaves.

They had given up any hope of swimming in the pool while Blashford and his friends were there but their day out had suddenly become more of an adventure. They decided to get a good spot by the river where they found the clothes and wait to see what the three bullies would do when they realised their clothes had disappeared. Not to be left out of the fun, Timmy had taken one of the long scarves and trailed it some distance away from the rivers edge. It had got tangled up around an exposed shrub root when he decided to leave it there.

The children took up their positions behind nearby trees and waited for the fun to begin. Wingy put Timmy on a lead to prevent him from showing himself to the bullies and told his friends that they must keep quiet under any circumstances as he didn't want them to know who had taken their clothes. They didn't have to wait long and they heard the happy trio laughing and joking as they made their way gingerly back to where they had left their clothes. They were in the nude and looked around anxiously for their clothes and towels but they were nowhere to be seen. When Lizzie saw them she was bursting to laugh at the naked trio but she had to suppress her urges.

"I'm sure we left them here" declared Wilson sounding somewhat puzzled.

They kept on looking around the spot but there was no sign of their clothes. Then Blashford found one of Barney Swanson's shoes and suddenly the truth dawned on them.

"Someone has stolen them" said Swanson trying to shield his nakedness with his bare hands.

Lizzie was tempted to laugh out loud but she knew they must not be seen to be linked to the disappearance of the clothes. She knew that if her eyes met Cathy's they would collapse into a fit of the giggles and the truth would be out. They all knew from experience that the likes of Blashford would report their loss to the police who would, without doubt, diligently pursue all clues on their behalf. They also knew that if the shoe was on the other foot the police would ignore their loss completely.

The five sets of laughing eyes were focused on the shivering bullies from behind the trees and Wingy was having trouble restraining Tammy. The sun had gone behind the gathering clouds taking the warmth with it while the breeze was increasing in strength and feeling cold.

"Someone had taken them" said Barney Swanson stating the obvious as the reality of their situation dawned.

They were now acutely aware of the fact that someone had taken their clothes and were probably, at that very moment, watching their naked antics. They realised they were too exposed by the river and decided to take cover under the nearby trees.

Wingy saw the dangers and signaled to the others to remain quiet and retreat, tree by tree, further back into the woods. They were soon at the point where they had entered the woods and it was the signal for the girls to give free reign to their feelings. Lizzie looked Cathy in the eyes and they collapsed into delirious laughter. After all, the three bullies hadn't been challenged by anyone but had been brought down to reality by being stripped naked and not being able to do anything about it.

"That'll teach then" Cathy blurted out uncompromisingly as the boyish naked images danced in the forefront of her mind.

David drew one of the school caps from his pocket and tried it on for size. It had Wilson's initials inside but he vowed to scrub them out.

By this time, the weather had turned cold leaving Blashford and his pals at a loss as to what to do next as they shivered in their bare skins. They waited for someone to come past to get a message out to the police but nobody turned up. They got to the edge of the north end of the woods and shouted to anyone from behind the trees. They had almost given up when two elderly ladies appeared making their way home. At first, they thought the naked figures were people who were not right in the head and were some kind of sexual deviants but the boys hollered for help.

"Someone took our clothes while we were swimming in the Bluebell Pool and we're freezing cold" Wilson informed them from the cover of his tree.

"We need some help to get home Mrs but we haven't got anything… we haven't got anything to wear" added Swanson sounding very desperate.

"How many of you are there?" asked one woman trying to assess the extent of their dilemma.

"There are three of us and we are all from the Kings Grammar school" said Blashford hoping such information would convince the ladies of their good characters.

The women could see the boy's dilemma and they asked them their names. They called their names out and the women were more attentive now.

"Mrs. Swanson's boy:"

"Yes… from Denton Avenue" Swanson replied hopefully.

"Oh, I know who you are now… Wilson and Blashford: I'll let your mothers as soon as we get home so don't go away" she warned…

They waited for another three quarters of an hour then a car drew up and two people piled out.

"Barney? Ian? Francis? Where are you?" a boy's voice called out.

They recognised the voice as that of Eddy Aldridge, one of their school class friends. They answered feebly from behind the trees and Aldridge got three blankets from the car and closed in on them. Mrs. Wilson got out as the freezing boys emerged from behind the trees. She saw that they were in a pretty bad state and their teeth were chattering uncontrollably. She hurried them into the back of the car while Aldridge had to crunch up on the floor at their feet. Nothing more was said as the boys began to warm inside their blankets.

The car drew up outside Blashford's house and he was quickly ushered inside by his anxiously awaiting mother. Then Swanson was dropped off into the arms of his relieved mother and Eddy Aldridge went home. By the time the car reached the Wilson's house Ian had warmed up and his teeth had his teeth had stopped chattering. His mother sat him close to the fire while his younger sister made him a hot cup of cocoa. Mrs Wilson was itching to show her outrage at the person who took her son's clothes but she had to restrain herself until he was back to normal.

"Did you see who had taken your clothes Ian" his mother asked.

"Well no Mum we didn't see anyone and we had left them a short distance along the river away from the actual pool" he replied feeling quite stupid.

As for Blashford, he ended up with a severe cold and had to spend a week in bed.

The whole episode might have died a natural death but for the story breaking in the local papers. The article was accompanied by a photograph showing the face of a shivering and naked Blashford protruding from behind one of the trees. The story and the photograph had been submitted by the enterprising taxi driver who thought the episode had great merit and local human interest. It prompted members of the public to visit the woods out of curiosity, which resulted in all the missing clothes being found...except for Swanson's school cap.

The three bullies had learnt a harsh lesson in humility and had to keep a low profile in the coming months as one paper had made them out to look like fools for being parted from their clothes. It pointed out that, as pupils of the Kings Grammar School, they should have exercised a modicum of common sense and responsibility for their own well being which they clearly did not do. Needless to say, they had to suffer the skits and jibes, not only from other school pupils, but also from members of the general public. As for the five Holy Cross School children, they felt no guilt for their actions and were in no doubt that the bullies deserved all the ridicule that came their way. They were always reminded of their part in teaching the bullies a lesson whenever David wore his ill-gotten King Edward's school cap...

The End

Guard Dog's Court Order

As an old age pensioner, Mrs. Baines was becoming increasingly nervous about her safety. Her anxiety was the accumulative effect of the steep rise in the murders and muggings of old people in their homes. It was only yesterday that she read about an eighty one year old lady being brutalised in her own bed as part of a burglary. Although she didn't live on her own, her husband Harry was out for most of the day and came home after ten at night. That night, when Harry came in, she told him of her deep fear. He was very concerned and understanding and as she talked on, he was thinking of a solution to the problem. After some discussion, she mentioned a conversation she had with Tom Plumber of Tai Bach. He had suggested that she might consider getting a guard dog. Harry knew Tom Plumber since they were boys together and couldn't remember a time when Tom didn't have a dog. Harry agreed she should have a further talk with Tom regarding the best breed of dog to meet their requirements.

They lived in a pensioner's bungalow in the lightly populated area of the village. With the blessing of her husband, Mrs. Baines went to see Tom Plumber. It just so happened, that Tom knew of a litter of pedigree Alsatian pups. Mrs. Baines had heard somewhere that you should look for the weakest and puniest pup in the litter because they usually turned out to be the best dogs. When she saw the litter of eight she fell in love with them all but she had to choose only one. A deep maternal instinct welled up to the surface as she held each pup in her hand in turn. Finally, she decided to have the smallest one which seemed to be in a permanent state of torpor.

It was mousey in colour and had distinct flashes of white at its wrists and at the tip of his tail. She was thinking what to call it but decided to wait until she had consulted Harry. When he held it he commented on the fine texture of its fur. This gave Mrs. Baines the idea for a name, Tex. Tex settled down in his new home and as well as being a constant companion for Mrs. Baines he showed great promise for becoming a very good house dog. By the time Tex was four months old he was threatening to grow into a very big dog indeed. Each time he was let out on the green he took longer and long to return home.

One rainy afternoon, she was sitting by her fire with Tex at her feet when the doorbell rang. In a flash, Tex was up and at the front door. She had to close the dog in the kitchen before she was able to open the front door. A uniformed policeman introduced himself as Constable Herrick. After the preliminaries, the constable told her he had had several complaints about the Alsatian dog frightening young children in the area. Mrs. Baines vehemently denied the allegations and defended Tex at every turn. During these proceedings, the dog was going berserk locked in the kitchen. The constable went around the back to the kitchen window. When it heard the policeman the dog hurled itself at the window while Mrs. Baines tried to restrain him.

Before the constable left, he warned Mrs. Baines to keep the dog under control at all times. For a while afterwards, she took him out on his lead each morning for a short walk around the green.

That proved to be too sedentary for Tex who wanted to exercise his powerful muscles by romping, running and jumping. Soon, Mrs. Baines had to let him off the leash and it wasn't long before she fell back into her old routine by letting him out on his own every morning.

This went on for a couple of months without any trouble or complaints. Then one morning she received a court summons in the post. Harry had long since left the house for his part time and she was left to ponder on the official document and its contents.

"You are summoned to attend the Magistrates Court at 10am in the forenoon of Monday 2 March 1951 to answer the charge of being the owner of an Alsatian dog and allowing the same to run wild and out of control to the detriment of the safety of local people…." Before she had finished reading the summons she fell back into her chair stunned and disbelieving. Tex sensed something was wrong and he crawled over to her chair and muzzled her limp hand in a gesture of understanding.

She looked deep into his loving brown eyes and stroked his noble head. He stood up wagging his long bushy tail as he nose pointed towards the back of the door where his lead was hanging. Mrs. Baines remembered her hadn't been out for his romp but she now realised she must take him out on the leash. She took him a considerable distance from the house then let him off the leash. After five minutes or so he came romping back and she managed to put him on the leash again. They walked home at a slow pace and the dog sensed his mistress's heavy heart. That night, when Harry came home she nearly broke down under the strain.

Harry tried to find answers to all sorts of questions posed by the court summons. Eventually, they concluded that come what may, they would defend Tex's right to life. The dreaded day soon arrived and they duly presented themselves at the court. They had to wait around for two nearly two hours before they were called into the court. Against the far wall was a raised dais upon which was a high desk-like structure. On the wall behind it there was a huge royal coat of arms with the inscription underneath which read, "Duet mon droit" It looked very imposing and intimidating.

They were ushered to a bench in the front row then a voice called out, "The court will rise"

Three people entered from the back of the dais and took their places behind the high desk. A policeman read out the charges and the middle magistrate asked Mr and Mrs. Baines if they had anything to say. Mrs. Baines told the court that Rex was a very good house dog and yes, she did let him out on his own sometimes because he couldn't wait. Evidence was given by PC Herrick who also made reference to further complaints the police had received from local people since he had visited the Baines's.

Herrick voiced the local fears that it was only a matter of time before the dog attacked someone... possibly a child. Mrs. Baines couldn't contain herself and shouted from the well of the court.

"I'd like to know who complained to you because nobody has said anything to me about the dog" she said to the policeman.

She was fuming with rage and the blood had rushed to her head and the magistrat immediately reprimanded her'

"Any further outbursts like that Mrs. Baines and you will find yourself in contempt of court. Do I make myself clear?"

In the event, the bench decided that Tex was a danger to the public and an order was made for the destruction of the dog. The old couple arrived home defeated and heartbroken at the prospect of Tex's impending doom. As soon as the dog saw them he greeted them enthusiastically but they were both consumed with guilt. Two days later PC Herrick and a plain clothed man appeared at the door. Mr Baines knew they had brought the fatal order for Tex. Herrick introduced the other man as Sgt Mercer of the dog handler's squad. They eyed the dog up through the kitchen window the Mercer nodded his approval. Herrick then put it to Mrs. Baines that Tex would make a good police dog if she would agree to it. He explained that the police would apply to the court to have the destruction order set aside then the dog would be able to join the troop to commence training.

The End

A Revealing Route

It was Monday morning at the factory of Helton Electrics in Birkenhead and the day of the launch of TX17…the firm's new vacuum cleaner. It was an ambitious but necessary move for the firm into the civilian sector after being a manufacturer of detonators to the wartime Ministry of Defence. The Second World War had been over for only three years and TX17 was their first product outside the munitions field. For the purpose of marketing, the new vacuum cleaner was called the Smoothy of which there were four models. Before starting out on its first sales expedition Tom Ballard had an appointment at nine o'clock with Mr Leighton Farndon, the managing director. Ballard's department had already made good sales inroads into the market place through the trade press and the next five days would be devoted to direct selling and by confronting the dithering potential customers.

Ballard was received right on time by the managing director who explained the importance of the firm recouping its big financial investment in TX17and how the firm's survival was dependent on its complete success. Mr Farndon went over Ballard's proposed itinerary that was concentrated in the Midlands. Mr Farndon added possible new clients and made some useful suggestions. When they had finished Farndon shook Ballard's hand and said;

"I'll see you at nine o'clock next Monday morning with your report and I'm sure you'll be able to tell me that your sales drive was a big success"

Ballard thanked him and promised to 'open the clams' as he aptly described clients who held on to their money. As he left the office Mr Farndon said half jokingly;

"Oh, and try to go easy on the expense account"

Ballard couldn't decide whether this was a jocular quip or a warning not to over entertain.

His final destination for that day was Birmingham with various stops on the way. He carried two samples of each of the four models in different colours that took up most of the space in the firm's green Commercial van. He had two calls to make around Chester before heading south for his first call proper at Batcher's Emporium in Stoke on Trent. From there, he cut east across county to the head office of Edgar's Modern House Aids in Leek who had eleven outlets in the larger towns around the area. He had to deal with a Mr Ray Hammond who was Edgar's electrical manager and who put the TX17 through its paces. Hammond, who was an electrical engineer, was about thirty three years old and obviously knew his job. He had served with the Royal Mechanical Engineers during the war and came to Edgar's with glowing references.

After examining the machines with the aid of Ballard's technical manual, Hammond made two valid recommendations with regard to the basic electrical circuitry. "This wick not only improve its safety operation but would only simplify its production and bring down the assembly cost" he advised authoritatively.

He then stood back and surveyed from every angle.

"With regard to the overall design I am in no doubt that you have got yourself a winner here Mr Ballard but if I were you I would certainly incorporate those two recommendations. When you have done that I will be only too glad to market your product" he said frankly.

Ballard would certainly bring these points to the attention of Mr Farndon in Birkenhead and although he was disappointed at not making a sale there and then he had been very impressed with Ray Hammond. He drove back to Stoke on Trent for his next call at Newcastle under Lyme. He had calls on either side of the main road leading south which he had to clear before finally landing up at his hotel in Birmingham. Ballard had intended to review his day's work but he was so tired he fell asleep in the hotel lounge. Tuesday proved to be another hectic day as he traced a circuitous route taking in Bromsgrove, Redditch, Stratford upon Avon, and back to Birmingham.

On Wednesday he concentrated on Birmingham and made a point of finishing early so as to bring his ledger up to date. He had also arranged for five potential customers to come to the hotel for a demonstration and he remembered the managing director's jocular warning about the expense account. He was glad to turn in when he had finished and as he fell asleep he was thinking of two customers he hadn't been able to convince about the merits of TX17. Losing sales always hurt his professional pride but other than that it had been a very successful day and proved and proved to be a peaceful night.

He awoke early and refreshed on Thursday morning and after breakfast he paid his bill. He was soon on the road to Northampton with one brief call at Daventry. He felt more relaxed now that he was heading north again but was mindful of some tough selling between then and Friday evening. By lunch time he found himself in Market Harborough and was a little surprised that he was still feeling fresh and alert. There was no time to waste so he pressed on the Leicester where he spent the whole afternoon. His last call in the town was a single story shop of no mean dimensions that went under the name of Kean's Hardware. Ballard thought he had heard that name somewhere before and, being a commercial traveller, he probably had.

He carried one of the machines into the building and was directed to the manager's office. The man seemed to like what he saw and asked Ballard to wait a minute while he went to another office. Presently he returned with another man whom Ballard instantly recognised as Ray Hammond, Edgar's electrical engineer. The thought uppermost in his mind was that he could have saved himself the time and trouble had he known that Hammond was going to be the man he would have to see again.

"Well, well, fancy seeing you so soon Mr Hammond… and I haven't forgotten your recommendations" he assured as if meeting up with a long lost friend.

The unmistakable resemblance between this man and Ray Hammond was so striking that Ballard could have been forgiven they were one and the same man. Ballard wondered why the man wanted to see the machines again as he had already examined them thoroughly on Monday. The man however looked at Ballard as if he was simple in the head. It was quite clear now that this man had never met Ballard in his life.

The first thing that came to Ballard's mind was that Ray Hammond was running this business in parallel with his job at Edgar's of Leek and didn't want his boss to know anything about it.

"Do I know you?" asked the man in a puzzled tone.

Ballard, seldom lost for words, suddenly felt outflanked and self conscious. The manager recognised there was some misunderstanding then introduced him.

"This is our Mr Kean… the owner of this shop and he would like to see you demonstrate the Hoover before we go any further"

Ballard apologised to Mr Kean then sprinkled some confetti on the mat and proceeded to Hoover it up. The two men watched intently and when the carpet was clean Ballard said reassuringly;

"There, you can't do better than that. Can you Mr Kean?"

The two men were impressed with the result and nodding his consent to his manager Mr Kean left the room.

The manager placed a varied order for six machines and when the business was concluded Ballard said;

"Mr Kean is the spitting image of a Mister Ray Hammond who I met in Leek on Monday morning"

"Well it wasn't Ray you saw Mr Ballard I can assure you about that because I know for a fact that he was in this shop on Monday morning."

"Well, if he isn't Ray Hammond all I can say is that he must be his twin brother"

"As far as I know Mr Kean has no brothers or sisters" assured the manager.

"If you could only see his Mr Hammond you'd see what I mean"

"I think he would know if he had a twin brother don't you Mr Ballard?" the manager replied in his boss's defence.

Ballard thanked him for his business but he was still shaking his head in disbelief as he left the shop.

His next stop was in Nottingham so he decided that he had enough time to press on and stay the night there. This would give him an early start on the final leg of his journey home on Friday morning. By eleven o'clock he had clinched a further three substantial orders. His next call was 'Repairs and Spares' which was one of the leads given to him by his managing director.

In that regard, he thought that would be a feather in his cap if he could get a positive result from it. The doorbell tinkled as he entered the dingy shop but there was nobody there. He then noticed a curtained doorway leading to the work shop at the rear of the premises. Presently, a man holding a screwdriver and wearing a bib and brace overall emerged from behind the curtain. Immediately, Ballard's jaw dropped in utter amazement as he recognised the man as yet another Ray Hammond.

This reaction caused the repair man some unease and he asked nervously;

"Yes?"

Ballard was not going to make the same mistake a second time and handed the man his calling card without any greeting. The man read it and extending his hand introduced himself.

"How do you do Mr Bollard…I'm Harry Fallon… What can I do for you?"

It was too much for Ballard and all he could say while shaking his head from side to side was;

"I don't believe it…I just don't believe it. It can't be happening again"

Harry Fallon was just as puzzled now as he watched the expression of disbelief on Ballard's face.

"What is it you don't believe Mr Ballard?" asked Harry somewhat confused.

"Tell me that you have two identical twin brothers" pleaded Ballard.

"I'm sorry to disappoint you Mr Ballard but I happen to be an only child" he replied.

The thought struck Fallon that perhaps Ballard had sipped one nip too many from his hip flask.

"Are you sure Mr Fallon?" Ballard was compelled to press the question.

Fallon's patience was showing signs of cracking and he began to wonder what sort of a game Ballard was playing.

"I'm a very busy man Mr Ballard…" he began and sounded as if he was losing patience.

"…so if you would state your business perhaps we could get on"

Ballard had come to the conclusion that he must tell Harry of his meetings with Ray Hammond of Leek and Ted Kean of Leicester. It they weren't triplets they all bore a strong uncanny resemblance to each other and Ballard was in no doubt that they were brothers. He related the relevant parts of his business tour and before long his sales technique had convinced Harry that he must make further inquiries regarding Ray and Ted. Harry's curiosity was now irrevocably roused and he thanked Ballard and promised he would make further enquiries. Ballard was doubly pleased with himself as he had not only secured a substantial order from Harry but was convinced he had reunited three twin brothers. They parted on a hopeful note and Ballard went on his way wondering what tomorrow might bring.

Back at work on the following Monday Ballard reported to the Managing Director's office. Mr Farndon went through the sales ledger with Ballard and he was very pleased with his traveller's efforts. TX17 was on its way to becoming a sales success story for Helton Electrics and four more sales tours were arranged for other regions of the country…

It was about eleven months later that Ballard received an invitation from Harry Fallon. He was to come down to Stafford and attend a family reunion as the 'most honoured guest'. He would stay overnight at a first class hotel and all expenses would be taken care of by the family. The brothers had managed to make contact with an ageing Nurse Morley who had actually brought them into the world and had looked after them before they were separated. She told them about their mother Margaret who had never really recovered from the births and passed away when they were just ten weeks old. Nurse Morley even showed them the entry in her record book, which had the names of all the mothers and their babies in her charge.

It was from this book that the triplets learnt that their family name was Henderson and that they also had a sister called Peggy. As far as Nurse Morley could remember Peggy had been adopted by a young couple from Canada but she didn't know their name. The brothers had engaged an Enquiry Agent in Canada to track her down but they had heard nothing to date. They were for ever indebted to Ballard for his discovery when making his fateful journey the previous year and they promised to keep him informed of all new developments. Nurse Morley told them it had been touch and go as to whether the four tiny babies would survive and every effort was made to sustain them.

The sad news that came to light was that their father, Harry Henderson, was killed in France while serving with the Gloucester regiment in the Great War and he never saw his children. These were the circumstances which prevailed at the time and which brought about the separation and adoption of the four babies to by four different families.

The End

Thou Shalt Not Covet

David had entered the kitchen just as Lydia was stretching forward across the Aga cooker to lift a heavy pan of boiling stock water.

"Ooops: don't try to lift that my dear, it is far too heavy for you" he said. She did as she was bid, looked at David and smiled. He took hold of the pan and asked her where she wanted it.

"Well, I was going to put it over in that corner" she told him.

"There now, and please Lydia, don't try doing heavy things like that. You know you are far too frail for that sort of thing and you know how it hurts me to see you trying" he said from beneath a furrowed brow.

They had been married for three and a half years and his love for her was still as strong as ever. Lydia knew that deep down he was a very jealous man and there was nothing he wouldn't do to keep her. The truth was that he always tried to be considerate towards her but there were times when she felt his attentions were stifling and overwhelming. She would try to tell him, via her big brown expressive eyes, that she really could do things for herself but he was blinded to her feelings by his own ego. It didn't seem to occur to him that she might like to have her own space… to do her own thing… but she didn't want to upset him. Nevertheless, his attentions often bordered on being oppressive and she wondered if he could tell the difference between them. She decided to go out and break the monotony and spend some time just window-shopping.

She was taken by a display in Graham Dunne's shop window when she felt someone tugging at her coat. She turned around and saw it was her old school friend Julia Stafford. They were very good friends until Julia's family moved away from the district some time earlier.

"I wasn't quite sure it was you Lydia…with your new blond hair and that" said Julia.

"Well, what a surprise to see you Julie although it did say in my stars that I would meet up with an old friend today" she said.

"Here, I don't mind being called a friend but old… now that does worry me" They decided to go for tea in Maxine's Café.

After talking about old times Julie said,

"I'm getting engaged and I'm having a party on the sixteenth of June… I'd like you to come" said Julia.

"Well I'd be delighted to go but what will my husband think" said Lydia conscious of his probable reaction.

"Good God Lydia, do you still worry about what David will think? You're his wife not his slave and you have a mind of your own.... don't you? It seems that every time you think of doing something you automatically have to worry about what David will think. That's no way to live...now is it" said Julia.

"Well he's all right but he does get jealous and I...."

"Never mind what he thinks... just tell him you're coming to my engagement party and if he doesn't like it he can lump it" said Julie decisively.

"Besides...." she added, "....you want to tell him he can think what he likes because only him has to live with his thoughts"

Lydia always admired Julie's attitude to life and often wished she had something like that in her own nature. Her decisions, more often than not, were made by other people even though she didn't realise it at the time.

"Who else is going... to the party I mean?" Lydia asked inquisitively.

"Well, the list isn't complete yet but... I'm sure it will turn up some surprises" she replied with more than a hint of mischief in her voice.

"Sounds exciting Julia and I really would like to come"

"Well then, use your head and tell him anything until the last possible moment and don't tell him where the party is being held... just keep him guessing" Julia advised.

"But he'll start asking me awkward questions and I...."

"Never mind that, I'll arrange for someone to call for you and he won't start on you in front of strangers" Julia told her.

The day of the party arrived and at the very last minute Lydia told David that she had to go out and that her two friends were calling for her. He began asking awkward questions but Lydia kept her nerve. Just as he was beginning to press for answers a knock came on the door. It turned out to be Gillian Hayes and Margaret Timms who had arranged to come for her and to deter David from making a scene. He seemed quite satisfied that the three of them were only going to a friend's birthday party and that they would look after each other. As soon as they were around the corner they piled into Tom Daly's waiting car and sped off to the function hall in the Meredith Hotel. The place was already lit up and the music could be heard outside. People were milling around inside indulging in small talk when Julia emerged from an anteroom.

"Well, you finally made it Lydia and I trust you told David a good story" she said while hugging her old friend.
"It was easier than I had thought it would be" she confessed.
"There you are then, you have been worrying about nothing, after all, haven't you" said Julia.
Julia moved on to other guests and Lydia sat at one of the tables around the sides of the hall.

By now the room was filling up with cigarette smoke but nobody seemed to notice it. Lydia was joined by a group of friends from her younger days and everyone was in a merry mood. There was no shortage of drink and Julia's sister Ellie kept the glasses charged. Lydia wasn't a drinker as such but the little she did drink made her a little tipsy. She had shed much of her 'shyness' but whether it was as a result of the drink or because she was among understanding friends was a matter of debate. She was determined to enjoy herself while she had the chance and renew old friendships and acquaintances.

The music was non-stop and feet were tapping as the room became stiflingly hot and stuffy. Then, a cool breeze swept through the room as someone opened the front door. Julia looked towards the door when suddenly a man appeared. She watched him as she thought she recognised him from somewhere. He was with two other men and the three of them immediately made their way to the bar. Suddenly Julia recognised him as Bart Hessle who used to be her boy friend. He looked more mature since she last saw him and his facial features had accentuated into the face of a man.

She recalled how much she had wanted to be with him and how much she wanted him to love her. Things had been going well when suddenly and without telling her, he had left the district. She couldn't make out why he had gone but she blamed herself for not yielding to his urges and expectations. The three men seemed to be deep in conversation then Bart made his way through the dancers. He seemed to be looking for someone but she couldn't be sure. He stopped once or twice to say a word to old acquaintances then moved on. He emerged from the dancers and his gaze fell on Julia. In that split second he thought he recognised Julia's face and after a moments hesitation he knew it was her. His face lit up as he came over to her table. In a flash he knew what he had to do.

"Would you care to dance Madam" he asked [coolly] while taking her by the arm and leading her on to the dance floor.

He drew her closer to him and gently kissed her on the cheek.

"Well I never expected to see you of all people Julia" he said pecking her on the cheek again.

"It's been a long time Bart" said Lydia looking up into his deep blue eyes.

He drew her even closer to him and, like putty in his hands; she moulded her body to the contours of his. They moved slowly as one around the floor thinking of what might have been.

"Are you married yet Bart..." she asked nervously.

"Yes I am Lydia and we have a small daughter Jade" he told her but he suddenly realised that telling her that could prove to be a mistake.

"And you Lydia, are you married?" he asked wanting to level the field.

"Yes… I'm married to David and we have a two year old son Jason"

"My word, you've been busy then" he said looking down into her brown eyes.

She smiled up at him and couldn't help thinking…. look who is talking.

The music stopped and he took her by the arm and led her back to her table. Her friends made room for him and he sat next to her. He felt he and Lydia had so much to talk about but it was going to be impossible with these people at the same table. The band started up again and taking her hand, he led her back on to the dance floor.

"You've got lovely brown eyes… like a horse" he teased but she smiled at him and knew what he meant.

"You know something Lydia, I should have married you. I think I've always been in love with you" he sounded sincere.

"Well, I was there in the garden that summer… in bloom and ready for picking so you did have every opportunity but alas… you passed me by…"

"Yes I did and perhaps you're right… but would you marry me now if you had the chance?"

She was suddenly thrown by this question and her whole being stiffened as she thought of the possible implications. Yes, David was a good husband as husbands went but he was far too oppressive which curtailed her freedom when it came to her self-expression. It was only then that she thought that David was nothing more than boring. On the other hand however, Bart was outgoing and exciting and could hold his own in anyone's company. Perhaps she would be happier with….

"Well, would you marry me now if you had the chance Lydia?" his voice had cut across her thoughts.

She hesitated to answer and smiled up at him while desperately trying the think of an answer.

"Well Lydia, would you?" he persisted while detecting the doubt in her voice.

"Well, there's no answer to that Bart since it could never happen"

"There's no such thing as never if you really wanted something to happen Lydia" he said positively, hoping to exploit her doubts.

She smiled up at him again but she couldn't think of the right words that would convey her true feelings. She could see all kinds of hurdles ahead if she made up her mind to go with him and, could she be sure that it would work out as they anticipated? She began to believe that fate had taken a hand in their lives and that she and Bart were meant for each other.

"I might, who knows?" she replied hoping to keep the door open"

They began to meet in secret and their love for each other blossomed. They soon began to experience an ecstasy they had never felt with their married partners and they knew they had tapped into, what poets might have described as, true love. Lydia's conscience troubled her and the secrecy of her affair with Bart nagged at her mind. Her husband knew, by her growing absences from home, that she had found a lover and that he had lost her. The new circumstances had also changed him and his frustrations were driving him to irrational acts of cruelty. Lydia mentioned to Bart that she was thinking of divorcing her husband then, to her surprise, he admitted that his wife had already filed for a divorce.

Lydia thought that fate was taking a hand in their affairs and had recognised that her first time marriage was obviously a mistake. She took heart from this and the fact that Bart was taking and set about putting her heart and soul in the new relationship. Bart moved all her personal belongings and little Jason's clothes and toys to their new flat. It all seemed like a dream now that they were alone in their own love nest and the future looked rosy. Even the children, Jade and Jason, had bonded like brother and sister.

There was lots of work still to be done to bring the flat up to standard and lots of nick-knacks and odds and ends to unpack. As she was unpacking one of the tea chests of her personal belongings she came across her late mother's family bible. She lifted it out and it fell open at the Ten Commandments. There was a passage highlighted in red which caught her eye and her curiosity prompted to read it.

"Thou shall not commit adultery. Thou shall not covet thy neighbour's goods nor covet thy neighbour's wife …"

Well, fate hadn't fully endorsed her liaison with Bart after all, she thought…

The End

A Good Feeling

The man was lanky and gaunt and looked older than his years. His clothes were ill fitting and his trouser legs fell short of reaching his ankles that appeared to accentuate his height. His back was stooped and he walked with the aid of a walking stick and was carrying a hold all bag which he held close to his person. The bag looked bulky but didn't seem too heavy and probably contained an extra garment in case the weather changed. He looked tired as he walked along the path towards the vacant park bench ahead of him. Two young boys in short pants and without a care in the world, brushed past him playing 'catch me if you can'. The ginger headed one had a prominent red birthmark on his right chin but it obviously didn't worry him. George was reminded of far off days when he was their age and it brought a pang of sadness at the thought of them having to grow old. He sat down on the bench and sighed with relief as the weight was lifted from his bony legs and he drew the hold all closer to his person…

He was thinking of his last consultation he had with Mr Affal Sidique, his specialist in the hospital when he delivered the prognosis.
"You are suffering from advanced cancer of the liver Mr Farmer and, you should errr… how should I put it…"
"You mean… its curtains for me doctor" he interjected.
The surgeon had hesitated then composed himself.
"Well, I wouldn't have put it quite like that Mr Farmer. Rather, I was going to gently advise you to put your …earthly affairs in order while there was still time"
Mr Sidique had waited for an adverse reaction but George Farmer never turned a hair.
"I see… what you really mean is that I am going to kick the bucket. Is that right?" The specialist nodded and George continued.
"We all have to go at some time doctor but many people are luckier than me… they go just like that. One minute they are with it and in the next moment the light goes out… just like that" he said snapping his finger and thumb together.

The doctor was surprised at how calmly George was on the uptake and secretly admired his down to earth attitude. He had delivered bad news like this to his patients on several occasions before but, he couldn't remember ever provoking a reaction quite like that.

"As a doctor, you must have seen some sights when you have had to tell people that they were going to die" George said.

"Well yes I have Mr Farmer but, in most cases, I only confirm what the patient already knows… or suspects" he replied defensively.

"Besides Mr Farmer" he continued…

"I have had patients who have made their own diagnosis and have worried themselves sick when I have had the pleasure of telling them that there was nothing wrong with them at all" said Mr Sediqui.

"Well doctor, I have been an alcoholic for far too long and I knew that I would end up with pickled livers sooner or later" said George as he held his hand out and said,

"Well thank you for all your help and advice and good-bye doctor. You tried your best for me but at the end of the day I knew you were only a doctor and not a magician" he said as their clasped hands parted and he left the hospital to face a short bleak future…

The two young boys came running towards the bench and they had now been joined by three others. They seemed to be out to use George as a hiding place from each other as if he wasn't there at all. He tightened his arms around the hold all and pressed it to his person as the two boys hid behind him.

"There they are Billy" said one excitedly.

George felt as if they were talking down his ear and wanted to tell them to go away but then he realised he wasn't going anywhere.

"Oh look Tommy… get down… they're looking this way but I don't think they have seen us"

George felt the same surge of excitement as the boys and he kept perfectly still. He could have stood up and walked away thereby blowing their cover but he imagined he was a member of the gang and wanted to play his part in the game. He felt Tommy inching up his back

"Get down Tommy or you'll give us away" said the other as he peeped over Georges shoulder to see where the chasers were. George could feel the excitement and tension in the other boy's voice and felt Tommy's hot breath on the nape of his neck as the chasers approached the bench…

The effect of the drugs George had taken was wearing off and the pain in his liver was getting worse. He didn't really want to move from the bench but there was no peace being used as a shield for those boisterous youngsters. It was time to move away for a more peaceful spot and as he stood up to go he felt his knees creaking under his weight.

"Ah aye mister, you've moved and they've seen us now" said one of the boys sounding miffed.

George was tempted to reply that if he had known he was playing hide and seek with them he wouldn't have moved. The chasers surrounded the bench and the boys were back to square one. George clung tightly on to his hold all and moved away towards another bench facing the lake. A woman sitting there moved to the end to give George and his bag plenty of space. She tried to weigh him up and put him into a pigeonhole so to speak but she couldn't make head nor tail of him. In any case, she had only come out for a quiet sit down to think of some way that she could leave her garrulous husband as she was at the end of her tether with him and was fearful of going back...

Neither of them said a word and the woman was beginning to feel self-conscious. The ducks on the lake swum towards their seat and the woman wished she had brought some bread for them.

"I hope the weather holds out" she said hoping to provoke a reply.

George had other pressing matters on his mind and he stared vacantly far out across the lake to nowhere in particular. The woman wondered if he deaf or if he was one of those ignorant people who thought they were a cut above everybody else. Then suddenly, George cried out with pain and clutched at his side. The woman was alarmed but quickly realised the man was in agony and stood up to give him more room. He was writhing with pain and she lifted his legs up on to the bench and put the hold all behind his head. She was surprised it didn't weight much as his head sank into it.

"Shall I call an ambulance for you mister" she asked.

George tried to get his breath to thank her but the pain was getting increasingly harder to bear. The woman summoned a passing couple and asked them to hurry and call an ambulance from the phone box half way around the lake. She turned her attention back to George whose pain seemed to have subsided for the moment. His eyes were closed, possibly with relief from the pain.

"The ambulance should be here very shortly but don't worry, I'll stay with you" the woman assured him.

George opened his eyes and tried to speak. The woman bent down to hear what he was trying to say.

The man took hold of her arm and drew her closer.

"Thank you… for all your help… and kindness my dear and I want you to have this… this hold all for taking the trouble to look after me. I won't… need it where I'm going… now promise you'll have it?"

His voice faded to a whisper and his eyes closed again as the sound of the ambulance came closer.

"There now, you'll be in safe hands and don't worry about your bag… I'll look after it for you" she assured him as the ambulance came to a stop by the bench.

The first man lifted George's eyelids and turned to the woman.

"I'm afraid its too late Mrs.…your husband has gone" he told her.

"He's dead all right misses" confirmed the second man.

She wanted to tell them that he wasn't her husband but the men were too engrossed in their work. By this time a group of people had gathered around as the men lifted him into the ambulance. They realised he was on drugs and searched his pockets to see if he was carrying them. They found papers that identified him as George Farmer and an appointment card to see a Mr Sidiqui at the General Hospital dated for the previous day. They knew that Mr Sediqui was a well-known specialist at the hospital and that Mr Farmer must be well documented on the hospital records as one of his patients.

The woman told them what had happened and they took him away. She then noticed the hold all on the bench and took charge of it. The ringing of the ambulance bell gradually faded and she sat down wondering what to do with the bag. She unzipped it and saw that it was something wrapped in plastic. It began to rain and she pinched a hole in the plastic and concluded it was a bag full of paper. She checked the time and saw it was coming up to five o'clock. She should have been at home by then as her husband would be waiting for her. He was the bullying type and expected her home in time to make his tea and wait on him hand and foot otherwise a big row was liable to ensue when she would have to suffer an incalculable number of insults. For quite some time she had considered leaving him but she had nowhere to go and no means of support…

"Why would he want to give me a bag of paper" she asked herself.

She wasn't going to carry a bag of paper around with her so she punctured the plastic and put her fingers through. She felt around then withdrew a few pieces of the paper that, to her astonishment, looked like

£50 notes. Automatically, she put her arms around the bag to protect it as she looked closer at the pieces of paper. She took some more from the bag just to reassure herself that it was indeed all money. She decided to find a more sheltered spot where she could count it and sort it out into bundles.

As she walked along she realised she was heading in the direction of her home only half a mile away but that was not a good idea. The less her husband knew about it the better so she decided to go into the ladies toilet in Woolworths to get a clearer idea of what she was dealing with. She counted the notes out in stacks of one hundred and was interrupted twice by someone knocking impatiently on the door and demanding she should hurry up. After the final count she realised she had thirty five thousand pounds and doubts as to her legal ownership of the money began to settle in. She stuffed several notes into her purse for immediate use as she thought the matter over. The thought struck her that it was her duty to deliver the money to the police but she quickly reminded herself that it was the man's last wish that she should have the hold all and its contents.

Why, he had even insisted she made a promise to take the bag for herself and that was before she knew it contained money. It could have just as easily turned out to be the man's dirty washing or something just as mundane but...a promise was a promise. However, she now had the problem of getting it home without her husband finding out about it but that was going to be difficult. She then came up with the idea of putting the bag in a left luggage office for safe keeping until she had a clearer plan. Not only that but she could take it out from time to time and take some money out then put the bag back. There was the possible prospect of losing the ticket but she vowed to put it in a safe place.

The system worked well for a while until she got the feeling that the two people who worked there were becoming suspicious. Every time she went to take some money out she thought she was getting some funny looks from them that unsettled her. She became more uncomfortable with the ready cash sitting there for any of the staff to help themselves. She decided to take the lot out and hide it at home while she fed it into a bank account in measured amounts and at respectful intervals. It took time and patience to complete the transfer but it was worth it. She kept the bankbook on her person at all times which bolstered her self-confidence and which didn't go unnoticed by her husband. She was her own person for some time into the near future and it was a good feeling… while it lasted…

The End

Dulce Domon

Binty Middleton moved with her baby son Frank to number twelve, a mid-terraced house in Padua Street in the small town of Latchem Green. She wasn't the gregarious type but, under pressure from her new neighbours, when asked about the boy's father she told them, reluctantly, that he had thrown her and her son out of the family house and that was how they ended up moving to Padua Street. The neighbours felt a great deal of sympathy and understanding with her plight and admired her quiet stoicism in coming to terms with her misfortune. They realised that 'there but for the grace of god….'' it could have happened to any one of them. They were all well aware that this wasn't an uncommon situation for wives and mothers to find themselves in; especially when they realised they were married to cruel and philandering husbands. They respected Binty's desire not to talk about her ordeal and were content enough just to know the broader details of her husband's cruelty. The question was seldom raised again and she was left to keep her bad memories at bay.

Binty settled into the close-knit community and began to build up a clientele for her seamstress work that tended to keep themselves to themselves. That was easy while Frank was a toddler but before long, he was old enough to go to St Anthony's local junior school. His mother would walk him to the school gates every morning until she was satisfied he had the confidence to go on his own. Naturally, his new class mates wanted to know all about him and his family. He told them how he and his mother had been thrown out of their home by his cruel father. At least, that was the story his mother had told him and he had no reason to question it. The boys had only recently witnessed the trauma, the heartache and the uncertainty when two of their school mates, the Fernley brothers and their parents, had suffered a similar fate at the hands of their landlord. Mr Fernley had broken his leg and his employer had no further use for his services and the rent fell into arrears…

His school mates understood how Frank must have felt and he was proud to tell them that his mother had scrimped and saved to buy her mid terraced house so that she wouldn't find herself thrown out into the street a second time. The boys saw the Middleton's plight as a battle between 'David and Goliath' and their boyish sympathies were generally with 'David'… the underdog. Indeed, as time went on, Frank witnessed other tenants and their families being thrown out of their homes by court bailiffs at the behests of their landlords and that fear was always at the back of his mothers mind.

Padua Street was a poor neighbourhood but Binty, fearing she could be evicted just as easily, had decided she wanted to be her own mistress as far as her home was concerned. Frank told his school friends how she had scrimped and saved and how they had done without the occasional treats and luxuries so as to accumulate the deposit to put down on the terraced house. In spite of the hardships, Frank had nothing but fond and happy memories of his childhood in number twelve and the thought of leaving it had never entered his mind.

The time came when Frank had to leave school and the question was what was he going to do with the rest of his life. He got a job right away as an office boy that surprised most people since he wasn't anything out of the ordinary as far as education was concerned. To add to the speculation, the neighbours learnt that he worked for Hale and Hale, a firm of brokers wheeling and dealing in such mysterious commodities as stocks, bonds, shares and futures on the stock market. Many believed Frank wouldn't adapt to the world of high finance while one or two thought he was definitely out of his depth. Some expected him to adopt lofty airs and graces to mask his academic inadequacies but such were alien to Frank's nature. Nevertheless, he seemed to take it all in his stride and went about minding his own business as he and his mother had always done.

He remembered starting work when his mother would accompany him to the bus stop every morning and see him off. She had even gone to the expense of buying him a new serge suit with long trousers, a white shirt and red tie. He remembered feeling quite grown up and full of quiet confidence in his new clothes. He now understood what his mother meant when she used to tell him that "Clothes maketh the man". Six months later she had saved enough money to buy him a new Gabardine raincoat… mainly to save his suit from wear and tear.

To add to his new circumstances, he fell into the habit of smoking 'Players' cigarettes. This was accepted as a sign of sophistication among the upcoming clerical class but Frank's excuse was that it gave him something to do with his hands. He once explained his reason for smoking as, if you can't beat 'em join 'em. He remembered when his suit was new and how the creased trouser turn-ups would flick against his ankles at every step reminding him of his new status as an office worker...

There was a clear perception between office and manual workers at the time and people tended to think in terms of 'them and us'. Of course, being Frank, it wasn't in his nature to see himself as someone more, or less, superior than manual workers but, at the time, office workers were expected to conduct themselves at all times with a measure of decorum. After all, they didn't dirty their hands, so to speak, as they were now members of the firm's staff. They would receive a pension when they retired as well as other perks and privileges and were often regarded as ambassadors of their companies to which they owed certain loyalties in return. Frank was quite content to do what was required of him to the best of his ability and never allowed his work to interfere with his home life. Over the next few years he made his mark in the commodities business and was soon acknowledged to be the whiz kid of the stocks and share markets. He was promoted to the board of directors to replace Erasmus Hale, one of the founder brothers who had passed on.

As time passed Binty, his mother, was feeling her age. She was now frail and for the most part, had taken to her bed. Reluctantly, but purely for the benefit and love for his mother, Frank put it to her that perhaps it would be better if she went into a nursing home but she wouldn't hear of it. He knew that she was as attached to the house and the memories it held, as much as he was. She simply told him that there was where she had made her bed and there was where she would lie in it. She agreed to have a nurse calling in three or four times a week to look after her medical needs and a woman to come in daily to do the cooking and housework but otherwise little else had changed.

The daily woman, Mrs. Ena Bantry, had been widowed two years earlier and had suddenly found herself in dire financial straits. She had applied for the domestic post and Frank Middleton learned she was thirty three years old and had four children still going to school. At the interview, she disclosed that her worst fear was losing the roof over her head and ending up in the street with the four children. Frank recognised the scenario all too well and saw in her a simple honesty and willingness to work. The locals assumed that, since Frank had been with the firm for so many years, they were footing his extra bills. Alas, his mother hung on to life, secretly hoping that her Frank would find a loving wife and settle down and produce grandchildren to keep the family name alive. As it turned out, she only lasted for another eight months and died in her sleep in the knowledge that there was no sign of her hopes coming to fruition....

Fifteen years later, at the age of fifty seven, the years were taking their toll on Frank Middleton's health. He had developed a pronounced stoop in his shoulders and had to lean heavily on a stout walking stick to prevent himself from falling headlong to the ground. He was still catching the bus at the same time every morning and puffing heavily on the proverbial cigarette. He was still wearing the same Gabardine raincoat that his mother had bought for him soon after he had started work. Like the suit, she had bought it two sizes too big then had taken it in at the sleeves and the hem so that it could be let out to keep pace with his rate of growth. As it turned out, he stopped growing when he reached five feet seven inches tall but by that time the coat had become his favourite garment. Over time, it showed some unprofessional repairs including ill matching replacement buttons.

Neighbours commented on his dowdiness and could only put it down to his low status at work. There was no doubt that his whole demeanour generated sympathy with the local people and there were the odd few who would have willingly helped or advised him on his dress presentation. At least, they conceded, he had a steady job and was apparently paid an adequate wage to enable him to maintain the roof, humble though it was, over his head and keep body and soul together.

The housekeeper, Mrs. Bantry, felt the old man couldn't afford new buttons and took it upon herself to buy a matching set and sewed them on. She had even replaced his worn shoelaces and sewn buttons on his shirt when required but she felt Frank hadn't noticed. She had the sneaking feeling that it took him all his time just to hang on to his job and assumed that someone at his place of work must have hinted to him at some time that he should smarten himself up.

On arriving at the terraced house in Padua Street one morning the housekeeper sensed that something wasn't quite right. To her surprise, she found Frank had failed to get up out of bed. She heard him coughing and went upstairs and knocked on his bedroom door. She entered anxiously and thought he looked ghastly. She noticed the sheet was bloodstained where he had wiped his mouth after each fit of coughing and knew he needed medical help.

"Would you like me to send for the doctor Mr Middleton?" she asked sounding apprehensive; but he wouldn't hear of it.

"I'll be [cough] alright if you will [cough] get me a cup of tea…. Mrs. Bantry" he replied between bouts of coughing.

Reluctantly she agreed and went downstairs to the kitchen. She still thought that, after he had drunk his tea, she could persuade him to have the doctor or the nurse visit him. As she reached the foot of the stairs with the tray her hands were unsteady and the cup and saucer were rattling. She climbed the stairs gingerly and felt relieved he had stopped coughing. She nudged the bedroom door open with her foot and looked over towards the bed expecting Frank to turn his head but there was no movement at all. She put the tray down on the side table and saw that his eyes were wide open.

"Here you are Mr Middleton; you'll feel better when you have drunk your tea" she said nervously.

There was no response, as Frank didn't move. He just lay there staring up into the far and beyond. Suddenly she got the eerie feeling that she was talking to herself and a cold chill ran down her spine. Gingerly she lifted his hand which was still clutching the blood stained sheet then let it drop limply back on to the bed. She was riveted to the spot as she realised the man had expired. She felt very uncomfortable just being in the same room as the deceased as it reminded her all too forcibly of her own mortality. She closed her eyes tightly and with outstretched arms she reluctantly drew the counterpane over Frank's face then hurriedly left the room…

Of course, he had long been part of the scenery of Latchem Green and the neighbours were genuinely saddened by his passing. They feared there would be a conspicuous absence of mourners at the funeral so they conspired with one another to fill the church pews with their friends and relatives to give him a good Christian send-off. On the day of the funeral service, they found St Anthony's church full to capacity and they couldn't understand what had happened. They even doubted if they were at the right funeral and had to ask questions of the other mourners as to who was getting buried. They were reassured that the deceased was indeed

Frank Middleton but the question remained, who were these people… where did they come from and were they related to him…

In a potted history of the man, the Latchem Gazette revealed he had died of pneumonia brought about by pulmonary complications. To many people's surprise he was only fifty seven years old when most thought he looked nearer seventy. He had been well known throughout the commodities industry as a very shrewd operator and was worth keeping an eye on. He had the uncanny knack of correctly forecasting the movements of stocks and shares and many sought his advice. Over the years, he had managed to acquire, through good business acumen, all the shares in the company including those held by the Hale Brothers estates. After his will was proved in probate it transpired that he had left a staggering £2.500 000

People were left bewildered as to why a man with so much wealth would have wanted to live a life of such frugality and apparent loneliness when he could have had everything he wanted. Nobody seemed to have stopped to think that perhaps that might have been the way he wanted it… inconspicuous… peaceful and quiet.

[After some discreet inquiries they learnt that Frank Middleton had been quite a ladies man in his time and had sired at least as many as twenty three children with as many women…]

The hearse carrying his body arrived at the church followed by a single limousine that carried the six coffin bearers and the funeral director Mr John Duggan. Duggan was well known for miles around for his pomp and decorum and for the outstanding dignity he displayed on such sad and solemn occasions. Of course, he was in business and his attention to details was reflected in the final bill for his services. He was met by Father Peter Mayer, the elderly parish priest and eight alter boys. It was unusual to see the elderly priest conducting a funeral as he wasn't too steady on his feet at the best of times and he certainly couldn't stand waiting around in the cold.

At the given signal Mr Duggan, who was well known for his punctilious bearing and dignity, led the funeral procession up the aisle. People were somewhat curious as to why the ageing Father Mayer should be officiating at this funeral as such services had long been the province of the younger members of the clergy. The coffin was followed by eight altar boys and the priest. The latter began to intone St John's gospel.

"I am the way, the truth and the light, he that believeth in me etc…"

When the coffin was rested on the bier, Father Meyer descended from the altar physically aided by one of the Deacons. He circled the coffin blessing it with holy water then faced the congregation and began the Introit to the Mass.

"In nomine Patris, et Filii, et Spiritus Sancti" he said blessing all those present.

There was a robust response from the people as they replied in unison…

"Amen"

In the next moment, the priest was reciting the "Confiteor Deo…" and everyone became aware that the Mass was to be conducted entirely in Latin. This was a turn-up for the book since the "Tridentine Mass" had been discontinued some years earlier as a result of an edict from the Vatican. Father Meyer had told Frank that he would have to seek dispensation from Rome to conduct such a mass but Frank insisted and said he would make it worthwhile for the church. It seemed that no expense would be spared for his funeral and he must have had a job persuading the elderly priest to conduct the Requiem Mass in the first place. It was more than likely that Father Meyer was the only priest in the wider district who could perform the ceremony since he was of the old school when Latin was a prerequisite to being ordained a priest but more importantly, for the celebration of the Holy Mass.

After the service, people saw a long line of limousines waiting outside the church. It transpired that Frank had been quite a ladies man on the quiet and had instructed his solicitor to write, in confidential terms, to twenty three women inviting them to his funeral. This was the first time each of them had learnt that they were not the only lovers who had shared a bed with Frank Middleton. Not only that but unknown to each other, most of them had conceived one or more of his children. Mr Duggan, the funeral director, ushered each of the self conscious ladies, some of whom were accompanied by their offspring, to her own limousine. This was typical of Frank Middleton as it was his charm and habit in life to treat each lady with his undivided attention. He would make each of them feel like a goddess and treat her in the same vane. To the ladies and the onlookers, the long convoy of limousines was a bizarre scene which drew puzzled looks and frowned foreheads. But Frank was anything but cynical and had never lived by the saying "… love 'em and leave 'em…" He had loved these ladies and all were invited to hear the reading of his last will and testament. They were all rewarded handsomely for "…bringing great joy and comfort into my life and I consider all of you as equal members of my Dulce Domon… my Happy home"…

The End

The Mystery Woman

The Morning Gazette was lying front page up on the mat beneath the letter box. There was a large photograph depicting police milling about outside a canvas structure. Prudence Redmond couldn't help reading the headline.

"Police excavate in copse after human bones discovered by man walking his dogs"

She lifted it up and gave it another cursory glance then went into the kitchen to put the breakfast on for her husband Oliver and their six year old daughter Harriet.

The little girl followed skipping into the kitchen and carrying 'Trupple' her trusted rag dolly. He had lost an eye when Casey, the cat, used to play with him when he was still a kitten. Since the attack, Trupple, who started out a 'Truffle' but the young Harriet found it easier to say Trupple, had always slept with Harriet so that she could protect him through the night. She sat him up in her old high chair and Prudence gave him his usual bowl of corn flakes. When he didn't eat it Harriet would take his spoon and coax him how to eat.

"Come on Trupple, you'll have to eat your breakfast if you want to grow up to be strong like Daddy"

In no time at all Harriet had eaten it all up just showing Trupple and to all intents and purposes the dolly had eaten his breakfast. Of course, she and her mother knew it was only a game but they played it with sincere reality.

Oliver Redmond was a successful engineer and businessman and was now managing director of Kadus Refrigeration International. The latter was an organisation with interests as far afield as food production to engineering and manufacturing which Oliver had built up from nothing. He had always been dedicated to his work even to the exclusion of a social life. The only continuous contact he had with the opposite sex was his mother and his loyal personal secretary Miss Prudence Germyn. When his mother died he became more reliant on Prudence when it came to questions concerning the business. Maybe it was because she was no oil painting that she too had no social life and as a consequence all her energies went into her work.

They were both in their late forties and Oliver came to realise that his life-long efforts in building his empire seemed pointless in the long term, especially if he was to die without issue. It was this train of thought which directed his attentions towards Prudence whom he had always trusted implicitly. Up till now, their relationship had been that of employer and employee and they conducted their daily working lives with measured decorum.

Oliver was a man's man through and through and recognised he lacked the social graces to talk to Prudence as a man to woman. He had agonised for some time as to how he might break through the barrier of their strict working relationship and allow him to touch on the question of marriage. He had tried to convince himself that she wasn't all that plain and that she would look more attractive if only she changed her hair style and dressed less like her late aged mother.

It had been a difficult time for Oliver but he finally managed to put the idea of marriage to Prudence. She was absolutely speechless at the suddenness of the suggestion. Almost immediately, Oliver wished he hadn't mentioned the subject as he became even more unsettled than Prudence. She realised he was as shy as herself on matters of the heart and, taking command of the situation, she persuaded him to sit down.

"I think it is time we both had a strong coffee Mr Redmond"
She hastened to the ante room and emerged presently with the coffee tray. She had always respected him for the way he made decisions when it came to business but this talk of marriage was as new to him as it was to her.

Once they had found common ground he was able to explain about the sterility of their efforts in making the business work if, in the final analysis, there was nobody to pass it on to. She saw the sense in that line of thinking but did he expect her to have his baby. They realised there was no affection of the heart between them but recognised that they had a deep respect for each other. They also accepted that that this could be a good stat to their 'new' relationship especially if they were going to live under one roof.

"You don't expect me to have your baby at my time of life do you Mr Redmond?" she asked with a hint of frost in her voice.

75

"Why certainly not Miss Germyn; I was thinking we might adopt a son but, I couldn't do it on my own… if you see what I mean"

"I suspect you already have trouble looking after yourself since your mother passed away Mr Redmond let alone trying to cope with a child"

Oliver detected a note of understanding in her voice. They finished the coffee and Prudence made another pot as they had a lot more to talk about. The consensus was that Oliver needed to adopt a son to inherit the business and they both had to understand that their marriage would be more of an arrangement with advantages to both parties…

Prudence adapted well to her new life and was surprised that she not only liked it but found that she still had that maternal instinct which she used to lavish on her dolls when she was a girl…

Little Harriet was coaxing Trupple to finish his breakfast while Prudence watched her from the corner of her eye. It was only then that she realised what a good job she had done in bringing Harriet up to this age. Harriet heard her father coming down the stairs and ran to meet him at the kitchen door. He swept her up in his arms and they hugged each other tightly. Harriet held Trupple forward and Oliver was expected to kiss the limp rag dolly. He sat down at the table and was joined by Prudence. He picked up the newspaper and once he had grasped the gist of the headlines and the photograph of the police he turned to the financial pages.

Late that evening there was a TV News update when Oliver learnt that the police had uncovered the remains of at least five people buried in the copse. Over the next few weeks, 'the bodies in the copse' story held the headlines and the police eventually revealed they already had a man in custody who was helping them with their enquiries. Oliver, like most business men, didn't dwell too much on headlines as long as they didn't refer to matters relating to business. Several weeks later, the man held in custody, a George Feeley, admitted to the murders of seven people and to burying them in the copse. Feeley, in fact, was already serving a life sentence for the murder of twenty four year old Florie Roach…

It was late in the afternoon on Friday when Oliver's office was winding down for the weekend when he received a curious telephone call from a public phone box.

"You don't need to know who I am Mr Redmond but I think you will be interested to hear what I have to say. I should tell you that what I have to say might pose a threat to your daughter Harriet if it was….." it was a woman's voice

Oliver had cut across the voice

"What the hell are you talking about and what do you mean it might pose a threat to my daughter?"

He felt unsettled and very angry that someone had the effrontery to broach his privacy. If anything threatened Harriet he had a duty to know and a duty to act.

"What is this thre…" but he was cut off in mid sentence.

"I know you wouldn't want the information made public so meet me at the Woolworths Restaurant in Sturt Melton at three o'clock tomorrow afternoon and remember, you should come alone" the voice said and the phone went dead.

For the next twelve hours Oliver dwelt upon the message from the mystery woman. He decided not to tell Prudence in case her worries filtered down to Harriet. Besides, wasn't it better to wait and see what the woman was talking about. He had toyed with the idea of informing the police but he decided that was a sure way of going public. Prudence guessed something was weighing heavily on his mind but she knew he would tell her if he thought it necessary.

Oliver arrived in Sturt Melton for 1.30pm and he had to drive around for some time before he found a suitable parking space. He then went to Woolworths, walked around the store for a while then decided to sit down in the restaurant with a pot of tea. By the time he had finished he looked at his watch and found the time had hardly moved on. Time dragged until a quarter to three when he sat down with yet another pot of tea. He kept watching the entrance to the café when he realised he didn't know who he was looking for. He could only conclude that the woman who had rung must know him by sight.

On the stroke of three a striking looking woman of about thirty seven came and sat on the chair opposite him. She was slim with a dark complexion and had straight black hair to her shoulders. He would have liked to see her eyes but she was wearing dark glasses. She must have been about five feet six or seven and he couldn't help thinking she possibly originated in the orient. He noticed a very faint small pale patch on the bone under her left eye. It was just clear of the dark glasses and he thought it might be a birth mark coming through her make-up.

"Mr Redmond? I'll come straight to the point. I am in possession of certain information which might jeopardise your daughter's happiness if it ever got out into the public domain"

Oliver watched her thin lips draw deeply on a cigarette as he tried to figure out what her motive was that brought her here.

"And what is this information Miss err…" he asked flatly.

The woman shifted [uneasily?] in her chair and leant forward exhaling smoke with a hiss.

"I'm afraid there's a bit more to it than that. You see Mr Redmond, I am here to disclose the information to you… for a fee" she said withdrawing a sealed envelope from her pocket.

"Aaahhh:" said Oliver as he began to get the picture. He continued;

"So this meeting is all about getting money out of me; am I right?"

She waited until the smile had fade from his face.

"I wouldn't put it quite like that Mr Redmond. You know as well as I do that good information, on whatever subject, commands a fee from one quarter or another" she was almost whispering as she continued.

"I would rather sell it to you Mr Redmond as it affects your family and your daughter in particular"

Oliver had been in similar positions such as this when dealing and negotiating with business suppliers and competitors where the price was the pivotal question but this present situation was quite another matter.

"And who else might be interested in buying this information?"

he asked hoping to penetrate the secrecy.

"I'd rather not go into that Mr Redmond as you will see the relevance to your daughter's happiness as soon as you know what it's about"

Oliver could see that the woman was getting slightly rattled and thought he was grasping the situation. He was used to knowing the name of the person he was talking to but it was unlikely she wasn't going to tell him who she was.

"Let me see now Miss errr… You have some personal information about my daughter and you want some money off me to keep you quiet and to keep you from divulging it to someone else. It that it:"

The woman nodded:

"That's about the size of it" she said.

"It has the foul smell of extortion and blackmail don't you think?" he said having decided to tackle her head on.

The woman didn't turn a hair and was obviously confident of her negotiating position.

"No blackmail Mr Redmond and no extortion. I have something to sell and I'm offering you the first refusal. It's as simple as that."

They were both silent while Oliver thought the matter over.

"Tell me Miss errr… how much money are we talking about?"

"Here are the goods Mr Redmond and I want £4000" she said holding the envelope at arms length.

"£4000 is a lot of money Miss errr…" he repeated as he thought hard on them matter.

"Tell me, suppose I don't buy it, who else is in the market for such information and do they think it is worth £4000?"

The woman was starting to get impatient;

"If you don't buy it then I will have to approach the tabloid press who may, or may not, pay that price for it. The upshot will be that the press will have a field day at your family's expense Mr Redmond and I'm sure you wouldn't like that for the sake of £4000"

Oliver juggled with the proposition in his mind and came to the conclusion that this woman had put a lot of thought into her plan. The money wasn't the problem for Redmond but he felt strongly that there was a principle at stake. What guarantee had he that this woman wouldn't take his money then sell the same information again to someone else? Besides, he might hand the money over and then find a blank piece of paper in the envelope. The truth was that, even the money wasn't a problem he had a duty to take any steps to protect Harriet from being hurt whatever the cost.

"Well, there it is Mr Redmond, take it or leave it" she said as she made moves to leave.

Oliver felt he was on a hiding to nothing whichever way he jumped so he decided to take the bait.

"Very well Miss errrr…I'll pay you the cash for what it is worth but I must warn you that you are dabbling in a murky business and if the opportunity does come my way I'll make you wish you had never heard the name of Redmond. Do you understand:?" there was anger in his voice.

"You have my word Mr Redmond that I will not attempt to sell the information to anyone else but if you try to find out who I am and how it came into my possession then I shall feel free to explore other interested markets" she replied sounding as if that was her last throw of the dice.

The woman sat impassively and stayed with the question of the money.
"I'll go to the bank with you if you don't mind Mr Redmond and I would prefer cash in used twenty and ten pound notes, if that is all the same to you"
Oliver hated himself for not being able to grasp the initiative except by way of paying up to find out what the envelope contained.

In the weeks that followed, Prudence noticed that Oliver seemed to have something on his mind and he showed it by being withdrawn and moody. He seemed to take a close interest in the news whether it was on the television or in the newspapers. As usual, Prudence wanted to ask him what was wrong but she had learnt to bide her time until he felt it was right she should know. On closer observation, she realised he was particularly interested in the "Bones in the copse" case. She didn't know that he was half expecting his secret to be splattered across the front pages of the press. Months had passed since he handed over the £4000 to the strange woman and his fear was that she would disclose the same information to the press.

He became more tensed when George Feely came to trial in the Crown Court charged with the murders of nine women and for the duration of the trial he was on tenterhooks. Feeley was found guilty of the heinous murders and sentenced to six life sentences to run consecutively. Finally, Prudence couldn't stand it any more ad asked him what was the matter.
"Remember that Friday, it was some time ago now, when that woman rang and insisted she had to talk to me?"
"You mean the one who wouldn't give her name?"
"You've got it: Well, I met her the following day in Sturt Melton and paid her £4000 for this" he said taking the envelope from his inside pocket and handing it to her.
Prudence took it and he saw the puzzled expression on her face. She withdrew the paper and read it while Oliver waited for her reaction. Her jaw dropped and the blood drained from her face as
she involuntarily crumpled the paper in her clenched fist. They
looked at each other for what seemed an age and she whispered;

"Do you think its true Olli?" she asked and the fear was evident in her voice.

"Well, whether it is or it isn't true the fact is that woman has got Harriet's date of birth right for a stat. The question is, can the rest of the information be right too?"

Neither of them wanted to repeat what was written on the paper but Oliver knew they had to face it together.

"If Harriet is the daughter of George Feeley we will have to do everything possible to see that she never learns the truth" said Oliver hoping Prudence would come up with something positive. There was another pause as he waited for her to speak.

"I always thought the details of an adopted child were kept secret… I mean, how did this woman get hold of such delicate information?" she said seemingly in a daze.

This was a valid point and Oliver figured his informant must have had access to social services and, or, the adoption agency's confidential files. If that was so, it shouldn't be too difficult to trace the identity of his mysterious woman he thought. But, and it was a big 'But' what was to be gained now by knowing the woman's identity? The answer might well be an even wider disclosure of Harriet's parentage and that would never do.

In the event, Oliver had discreet enquiries made of anyone who might have had access to Harriet's adoption files but none of them fitted the description of the mysterious woman. He learnt that only two people had left the social services in that time who might have had access to the adoption files. One was a tall gangly woman who had reached retirement age while the second was a man who left for pastures new and now ran a hotel on the sea front at Llandudno. He was about the same age group as his informant and was thought of as one of the pillars of the local society. He was the spokesman for the local Licensed Victualler's Association and one of the leading lights in the Little Theatre Amateur Dramatic Society. He wasn't married and strangely enough, stood about five feet six or seven inches tall… about the same height as the enigmatic woman. Oliver had finally come up against a brick wall and decided to let sleeping dogs lie. He abandoned his search for the mystery woman, trusting in her promise not to divulge any details of his little Harriet's birth details to anyone else. As time went on, he was haunted by the identity of the mystery woman and it played on his mind. It seemed she had disappeared into thin air and had covered her tracks completely. One day he got the preposterous idea that perhaps the man, who now ran the seaside hotel, might have something to do with the mystery. Ollie was prompted to visit the hotel and see if the man had any scar under his left eye but his face was clear. It was yet another brick wall but he couldn't help wondering… Suppose… just suppose… he thought, the man impersonated a woman and… Ollie suddenly feared he was drifting into the realms of fantasy and that his imagination was running out of control. He tried hard to dismiss the theory from his mind but the more he thought about it the more he realised it possible. After all, the man from the hotel was of similar age and about the same height and build but, in the absence of any other suspect, the man always came to mind when he thought of Harriet and her notorious parentage and frightening birth details.

The End